The Cryptic Tower

A Nunnery College Mystery

Geohn C. McAmby

VANTAGE PRESS
N

This is a work of fiction. The college on these pages is imaginary, with the exception of certain topographical similarities. The people, places and events are fictitious. Any similarity between the names, characters, and places in this book and any persons, living or dead, is purely coincidental.

Cover design by Polly McQuillen

FIRST EDITION

Copyright © 2005 by Geohn C. McAmby

Published by Vantage Press, Inc.
419 Park Ave. South, New York, NY 10016

Manufactured in the United States of America
ISBN: 0-533-14966-5

Library of Congress Catalog Card No.: 2004094250

0 9 8 7 6 5 4 3 2 1

To Dr. Constance Ruys of Menlo Park, CA

"Whereof what's past is prologue"
—William Shakespeare, *The Tempest,* Act II, Scene 1

For Mary Jo—
Just another literary
Effort. Enjoy!

Szahn C. McCamby

né
George

Acknowledgments

I gratefully acknowledge the advice, assistance and expertise of the following:

Cris Carter
Katharine Floyd
Michael McKinney
Charles Pitts
Marjorie Willingham
Libby Bailey
Ruth Weeks
Lisa McKinney
Donald Hamilton
Frank M. Whiting
Fedrico García Lorca
Louis Nunnery
Karen Renner
Emlyn Williams
Barbara Hall
Steven Spielberg
Jean Teems
Bernard Sobel
George W. McKinney
John E. Hamby
David O. Selznick
John Ritter
B.J. Goodwin

PART ONE

Prologue

The Camon Female Liberal Arts College for Women was chartered in 1850. (Incidentally, several institutions of higher learning were guilty of redundancy in the title during this period.) In fact, we celebrated our Sesquicentennial at the turn of the century.

A lot had changed during the 150 years. It became evident in the late nineteen-twenties that there was a need for the college to expand, but because of its downtown location, expansion was impossible. At what could not have been a more propitious time than in the early thirties, a local philanthropist offered the college the family estate of 240 acres west of the city. It was not known precisely what had spurred his interest in the college; it was thought that perhaps his mother or sister might have attended the institution. However, the prevailing opinion held that it was just his "stab at immortality."

The developing and moving to its new location began after the transaction became known. A 170-foot smoke tower was erected and steam tunnels dug as the dormitories and other campus buildings were being built.

By the early fifties, only the Fine Arts Conservatory remained in town. With the completion of the auditorium in 1955, the Conservatory concluded the move to its new facilities, and took steps to honor the agreement: the official adoption of its new name: Nunnery College (Although the oblique, though unintentional, reference to the gender of the students was not lost, the admonishment of "never look a gift horse in the mouth" was often heard.)

Caleb W. Nunnery had died in the late fifties. When his will was probated, after providing for the care and well-being of his sister and staff, the college received the bulk of the estate. It is not a sexist evaluation to say that Nunnery College was well-endowed!

An interesting institutional practice occurred when the college changed its name. From what we could learn, that from its origin, when a student, staff or faculty member was asked where they were enrolled, worked or taught, instead of replying "Camon," or the like, chances were that it would be "the Nunnery." However, when it took on its new name, the entire campus seemed to assume a protective mode and would respond with "Nunnery College"—emphasizing the institution rather than the gender.

Another matter had to do with student life at the former Camon College. Among the various clubs and sororities was an organization known as The Thomebeh Society. The name was an anagram and was probably as enigmatic as a Skull and Bones or a Gimghoul. In 1855, the organization was outlawed for reprehensible behavior and its members were banished. Without knowledge of the charges(s), we were surprised at the severity of the penalty. As a last resort, it was decided to search the archives in case the Thomebeh Society's escapades happened to have made the local newspaper.

Eventually the Thomebeh's anagram was deciphered as "Behemoth." I could not help but question why the Society had chosen this particular creature for its namesake. Since the purpose and function of the organization was vague, I wondered if the behemoth was a mascot or a symbol? If the latter, just what traits had they attributed to the beast?

If that weekend debauchery of the Thomebehs was indicative of the Society's agenda, perhaps they wanted the logo to be enigmatic rather than provocative. However, their indictments provide enough information for a possible scenario as to the origin of the Thomebeh Society. Since classical studies at the college would include philosophy, mythology, and drama, perhaps a group of students had been enthralled by plays such as *The Bacchae*, by Euripides. The drama is generally conceded to be an allegory opposing the forces of instinct and those of reason and wisdom, but perhaps the most memorable reference is to Bacchus, the god of wine, driving a chorus of women in a Bacchanalian madness. Becoming drunk from the wine, they tear off their clothes, and run wild over the countryside, slaughtering and devouring animals.

We theorized that perhaps the unconventionality of the revelry intrigued the group to the extent that it prompted the Society to try it. What we wondered, however, was whether that was their first orgy, or just the first time that they had been discovered. I also wondered if there had been repercussions to the College ruling, and if the Thomebeh Society had actually disbanded?

The possibility that a remnant of the Behemoths had survived was, for some reason, disturbing. We had not attempted to trace their activity since the arrest and expulsion, so we had no idea if the Society had continued to exist sub rosa, or what it might have evolved into. However, if there had been any sort of retaliation by the sorority sisters, Camon College archives made no mention of it. (Actually, a fire did destroy the old conservatory downtown, but that was after the college had changed its name and moved to its new campus.)

It seemed that our Sesquicentennial (directly or indirectly) was responsible for several changes in Nunnery College. Probably the most notable was the inauguration of the College's first woman president. She was responsible for funding two student apartment buildings and providing additional campus parking. The third innovation was hardly her doing, but since it was under her "auspices," she received the credit. Of all things, it was a state-of-the-art arena theatre to be built on the other side of Stetson Lake. However, it was the donor that was the mystery—and the surprise; it was none other than the Thomebeh Society that was now located in Camon. The reason for the offer was that the Society had been interested in our theatre program but felt that our 1150-seat auditorium was too large and that we should have a smaller, more intimate theatre. The Thomebehs offered to build an arena theatre if it were modeled after their mosquelike headquarters on the outskirts of Camon. We didn't particularly want an arena theatre, but the offer was too good to pass up.

During negotiations we did learn a lot about the Society. After their expulsion from The Camon Female College, the Society decided to become a benevolent organization and to remain organized as a society by passing membership from mother to daughter. In the absence of a daughter, a surrogate would be selected.

As soon as the apartments and theatre were completed, our first female president and her entourage departed and the position was offered to the Chairperson of the Board of Regents, who had been serving in an interim position. Although a Nunnery College alumna and a successful lawyer in Atlanta, she certainly deserved the appointment—but not the current crisis!

1

The topography of Nunnery College is an excellent example of a planned campus. All but one of its dormitories are clustered around the fountain in the center of the campus, forming three sides of a quadrangle. The senior dormitory enjoys the enviable location of being beside the six-acre Stetson Lake. The two new apartment buildings are on front campus. The administration building, with a common loggia, shares the north side of the court. There are two academic buildings, a new science building, the auditorium, gymnasium, library, art building, alumnae center, dining hall, infirmary, and across the lake, the Thomebeh Arena Theatre, the athletic building and the equestrian stables. The highest structure on campus is the 170-foot smoke tower located behind the physical plant. (The tower was the chimney for the furnace boilers that once supplied heat and hot water to the campus via steam tunnels.)

With its red brick facade and white columns, the campus reflects the best of Georgian architecture. Azaleas, Japanese magnolia, yoshino cherry, and ginkgo trees enhance the grounds along with native magnolia, pine and elm. The admissions office had always claimed that if it could get a prospective student on campus, she would want to stay.

An interesting feature indigenous to our "golden pond" was a ten-by-twenty floating botanical island. Upon checking with a biology professor and being informed that the pond was composed of alligator weeds, I inquired if it would support a body? She replied that it would not. (Should anyone entertain the possibility of say, discovering a corpse there, it would be necessary for it to be supported amongst the weeds like Moses in the bulrushes.)

As far-fetched as it may seem, this supposed serene *mise en scène* would provide the setting for one of Camon's most bizarre mysteries!

2

It was the first week of classes in the fall semester of Nunnery College and the campus was also involved in "Rat"—the traditional initiation that freshmen had to endure from the sophomores. The practice had been subdued over the years; however, a happening occurred during this particular week that would forever render the event in jeopardy.

Since freshmen were not allowed to have cars on campus unless they were bona fide residents of Camon and living at home, it was fairly easy to keep tabs on the new students. By Sunday evening, after Security had searched the campus, students, staff and faculty were notified with the name and description of the missing freshman.

Ashley Bowman was last seen Saturday night in the auditorium attending the final ceremony of "Rat" with her class and their nemeses, the sophomores. Ashley was an attractive brunette from Augusta, 20 years old and planning to major in theatre. In fact, she had auditioned for one of our scholarships during the summer. The fact that she was somewhat older than her classmates seemed to be an asset. Needless to say, I quickly became involved.

The search for the missing freshman continued into the following week. It was not known if she was responsible for her disappearance, or if she was a victim. I was assured that every nook and cranny on campus had been examined. Not certain whether the subject of investigation was a person or a body, an examination of her dorm room found nothing missing. I even rowed out to the floating island of alligator weeds—just as a precaution.

Although I was concerned about the plight of the student it occurred to me that if she herself had staged the vanishing act, Ashley Bowman was long gone!

3

I don't know how the most obvious structure on campus had been overlooked since every other storage bin and basement had been searched. As it turned out, our 170-foot smoke tower was the only enclosed area that had escaped scrutiny. Seated on a cement slab behind the physical plant, and once connected to furnaces supplying heat and water to the campus, it was now a 170-foot brick landmark with a fifteen-foot base, tapering to 6 feet at 170 feet above ground. Fortunately, there was a service door at the base for removing debris, and furnishing a connection to the furnaces. It was there that the body of Ashley Bowman was discovered two days later. However, she apparently had not been placed there: from the condition of her body, she had been *dropped* there! Although there had been rumors of bodies becoming part of the cement base of the chimney, this was the first evidence of a murder or a suicide.

I say murder or suicide because it had not been determined if Ashley had been thrown or jumped from the top of the chimney. In either case, there was the question as to how it was accomplished.

My father used to tell me that there were "human flies" who could scale brick walls by clutching the mortar between the bricks. By the same token, it could be possible to climb the wall by using suction cups on the hands and feet. Another far-fetched possibility would be to use a helium balloon, or a helicopter. The fall from the roof of the auditorium would probably be fatal; however, the interior of the smoke tower would provide seclusion.

4

Our campus security cordoned the site before notifying the coroner, who was accompanied by the Camon police. One of the first things that the new president had done was to upgrade the department by bringing in Jason Cabot, an ex-lawman. Nunnery College was fortunate to have had a trained investigator on its staff at this time.

While the coroner was examining the body, local police were making a cursory inspection of the area. The coroner's conclusion coincided with Cabot's, that the victim had probably "fallen" from a great height. He didn't speculate if it were voluntary or coerced.

After the coroner removed the body, I'm certain that Cabot and his crew went about their business of notifying the parents and checking on records and activities of the deceased. (At this time, we did not know if anything had been discovered at the scene.)

The autopsy came back within two days. It surprised me because of the condition of the body. I don't know why since so many "authentic" television programs such as *CSI* perform autopsies on embalmed and/or decomposed subjects. Of course, the Bowman family should have received the autopsy after the authorities, but for some reason, the family couldn't be located, so the College received it. There was no trace of drugs or barbiturates, she wasn't pregnant, but she was 30 years of age rather than 20. She apparently had no Social Security number, at least not under that name, and her fingerprints were not on file. Her high school transcript would be checked for verification.

The tragedy was a tremendous personal disappointment. Since I was slated to direct the first theatre play, I'd had Ashley read for the lead when she was auditioning for the theatre scholarship during the summer. I had selected Lorca's *Yerma* and since she was 20, I felt that she had the maturity to play it. Discovering that she was actually 30 made her loss even greater.

Federico García Lorca was a twentieth-century Spanish poet/playwright who was killed during the Spanish Revolution. His plays quite often were critical of native traditions that he felt were detrimental to Spanish culture. For instance, *The House of Bernarda Alba* depicts the tragic lives of five daughters who are confined to their home for 8 years when their father dies. In *Yerma,* the wife who is destroyed because her desire to become pregnant is so obsessive that she tries everything including a mountain orgy. My set design had an inner proscenium depicting a huge stylized pelvic silhouette through which the play would be viewed. If the audience recognized the symbolism, O.K. If not, it was still an interesting set design!

5

When an incident like this occurs, there is the guilt feeling that has to be managed. Concerning a student with whom you have had no contact, you wonder if you should have—or if you had, did you give too much attention to the matter? I was certain that I didn't tell Ashley that I was scheduled to direct the college's production of *Yerma* this fall. Of course, since classes had started, notices were posted on campus announcing auditions, and she could have seen these and remembered that she had auditioned for the leading role during the summer and did pretty good. While jealousy and/or competition of itself is dangerous, it was hard to believe that those emotions could be solely responsible for a student's death; but, despondency is difficult to understand and to accept. ... In spite of the seemingly limited activity atop the smoke tower, surely there are other theories than murder and/or suicide. Perhaps Jason Cabot and his crew would prove their worth.

The more I thought about the current tragedy, the more I thought about the obsolete smoke tower and the role it had obviously played. Surely the college would now have it removed, for obvious reasons? While the tower was a campus landmark, it would also be a reminder of the death of a student. Granted that it would be a major undertaking to raze such a structure, but I recalled that there were years when it was in need of extensive repairs for safety as well as cosmetic consideration. The surprise was that in spite of the many needs on campus, the college instigated an extensive renovation of the brick chimney. We were told that a bequest had been given to Nunnery College

14

earmarked for this particular project. Other than preserving a campus landmark, the rationale eluded us. At any rate, for the next several weeks, the activity on the scaffold and suspended platforms provided a source of interest for the local kibitzers and gawkers. It never occurred to me to wonder how the scaffolds, etc., were suspended from the top of the chimney. Was it possible that there was a metal ladder on the inside wall? If so, that would provide a way to ascend without being a "human fly," or using suction cups. However, my walk to the site found it still cordoned plus NO TRESPASSING signs. (Incidentally, I had eliminated a helicopter: too noisy—but I would ask Jason Cabot about an interior ladder.)

6

When Ashley Bowman applied for admission at Nunnery College, she listed Augusta, Georgia, as her home. The Registrar assumed that the transcripts that were received had come from the Augusta school system. However, since the college was unable to locate her parents, it discovered that Ashley's transcript, SAT, etc., were from Champaign County, Illinois, and they were dated 8 years earlier. Upon further investigation, it was found that she had been accepted at the University of Illinois at Champaign, Urbana, and had already received two degrees from that institution!

So—what was she doing at Nunnery College in Camon, Georgia, *as a freshman?*

I got most of the "in office" Registrar discovery from one of my "informants." I learned long ago that if you wanted to learn something, ask a student (or the mail clerk). It would seem that Ashley Bowman was some sort of an under-cover agent. In that case, suicide would probably be unlikely.

However, an interior ladder could be applicable to murder, but *only* if the subject is hypnotized to climb the ladder and then jump. . . .

7

I doubt if I could have been the only one wondering why Nunnery College was being investigated—especially when it was learned that Ashley Brown was older, with two college degrees. I didn't know what degree an "investigator" should have, since I didn't know what agency she was with: FBI, CIA, or perhaps a private or secret one? There are always campus activities that are humored other than drinking, pot smoking, etc. (A few years ago, there was even a fledgling prostitution club that was nipped in the bud before too much harm was done.) All in all, the last few years have been without incident. The students are either behaving or they have learned to keep it under wraps. Don't ask, don't tell; and don't delve too deeply. I heard several suggestions that investigators were "infiltrating" the wrong class: it is the upper class that causes the most trouble.

I was finally able to corner Jason Cabot long enough to ask about the smoke tower's ladder. There was one that went to the rim of the chimney and he agreed that it would be impossible to climb and transport a person to the top—even if unconscious. He did say that it might be possible to *hoist* a person to the top with a block and tackle, although he found no evidence of one.

We were now back to suicide vs. murder. As for the "modus operandi," suicide required only one person, while murder demanded at least two. Granted I am no afícíonado of mayhem and the like, but what about motive, opportunity, etc.?

Since Nunnery College now had a qualified security investigator, the Camon police paid only token attention to our conundrum. Although there was still no conclusion as to the crime's perpetrator(s), they seemed to be awaiting Jason Cabot's prognostication. In the meantime, the college attempted to resume its normal schedule.

8

Not unlike most single-sex institutions, the Theatre Department at Nunnery College was continually faced with the problem of casting its productions. We had just about exhausted the supply of all-women plays long ago, to the extent of presenting an "encore production" on more than one occasion. We have often been accused of casting anyone in pants—which is not necessarily true. Our male cast members are usually students' boyfriends, faculty members and available local talent. All in all, we have been very fortunate in assembling competent casts. I might add, that as a rule, we do not cast women in male roles—the exception being children's plays and perhaps nineteenth-century melodramas. However, we did cast women in *Oedipus Rex* a few years ago. Perhaps it was "poetic justice"—2,000 years late: in the fifth century, B.C., the Greeks cast only men in all of their plays. Although it was a tradition, one way that they got away with it was that the actors wore masks. We followed their example.

Our theatre staff is more like a family of three. While one is responsible for literature, one for costumes, and the other the technical aspects, we all wear more than one hat. We do four productions a year, which gives each the opportunity to direct one play—the extra one rotating. *Yerma* was to be the opening production, and it fell my lot to direct it. I was also responsible for the design—one of my many hats.

The auditions for the Lorca play were scheduled the second week of classes. Although *Yerma* had a cast of 28, fortunately 18 were female. Our opening play usually has a large cast since we want to involve as many students as possible. While we had presented *House of Bernarda Alba* a couple of times, this was our first attempt with *Yerma*. I was particularly interested in who if any had requested to read for the role of Yerma—just in case competition was involved in the Ashley Bowman demise.

To my relief, the auditions were without incident and I was able to assemble an impressive cast. However, it did seem odd that their classmate's fate was never mentioned.

9

There had been no further word from the coroner's office since the autopsy. All that we had learned about the victim was from the Registrar (indirectly) when that office located the source of her school credentials. It had been assumed that a student with two college degrees would not be enrolled in an undergraduate Liberal Arts College except possibly as a "plant" for some federal agency. If that had been the case, the campus should have been overrun with agents. Surely she would have been in contact with her superiors—probably by cell phone. I've never gone that route myself, but I understand that there is a record of all calls. As far as I knew, a cell phone had never been found.

I had just about decided that the information from Champaign, Illinois, was erroneous. However, we still had to contend with a murder—or suicide—of a 20-year-old freshman!

Every time that I started working on *Yerma*, I would start thinking about Ashley Bowman—about how little we really knew about her. I had already covered the assumption that she might be working for some Federal agency, since she was 30 years of age with two academic degrees, and enrolled as a freshman. I then began to wonder how she was identified at the bottom of the 170-foot smoke tower. Was she wearing an identification tag? (I couldn't remember if freshman wore them.) Was it possible that because a student was missing, and a body discovered, it was assumed that the body was that of the missing student? As far as I knew, she was "identified" by Jason Cabot's crew, who probably had only limited means to do so. There *was* a dead body in the Camon City morgue. It had been taken from Nunnery College—but it might not be the body of Ashley Bowman!

10

The following week, I blocked *Yerma* in the evening (telling actors when and where to move), and in the afternoons, began constructing the scenery. In addition to the pelvic-shaped false proscenium, the play required four inner sets. While the sets could be "suggestive," the extensive cast with its costume requirements would be responsible for a large part of the Theatre Department's annual budget. But in spite of its shaky beginning, Federico Garcia Lorca's *Yerma* was beginning to look promising!

11

The next week, the tech crew, coming to work, noticed water on the stage floor. There had been some rain the night before, and immediately the source of water was suspected: the access door to the roof of the theatre was open. Fifty feet above the stage was the gridiron, an open metal floor that supported the rigging system for flying scenery. The rule of thumb was that the grid should be twice the height of the proscenium arch, thus preventing suspended scenery from being seen by the audience when "flied." (A nautical term, not bad grammar.) The distinctive profile of a traditional theatre makes it easy to recognize on campus.

The grid is reached via a metal ladder, attached to the rear wall backstage. This ascends to the loft, a maintenance area between the grid and the roof. A short ladder leading to the access door and roof is reached by crossing the open metal floor of the grid. The view of the stage from this perspective is quite interesting—an effect that Hollywood has not overlooked.

I led the tour to the roof to inspect the cause of the open hatch. In the past, wind had been the culprit when the latch had not been secured properly. However, this area had not been inspected the previous week.

The roof is essentially the same size as the stage: 30-by-70 feet. A four-foot-high brick wall encloses the area, which also houses the giant speakers for the campus carillon. Rising over 100 feet above, it is second in height only to the smoke tower at the physical plant.

When climbing vertically to the loft, the novice investigators had begun to appreciate the slight incline of a normal ladder, and while crossing the grill-work, they had been awarded a bird's eye view of the stage. We discovered that the access door was open, so we made our way up the ladder to the roof. Every year I had taken the crew to the roof, not only to see the campus and the fall leaves, but also because this was one of the "perks" of being a member of the tech crew. I don't know what they were expecting to find, but it was certainly not what we encountered!

As I completed opening the door to the roof, I was accosted by the barking of a large dog. As the crew followed me, the dog seemed to be guarding an area near the center of the enclosure. We then heard a man's voice calling "Darya!" beside what appeared to be a lean-to against the speaker's housing. The dog ceased barking, and we approached the lean-to and the man who appeared to be heating something over a huge Sterno stove. Taking her cue from her master, the dog made friends with the members of the tech crew.

The man approached me and informed me that his name was Harry Selby, and that it was of course, a theatrical pseudonym for many reasons. After introducing myself and my crew, I remarked what a beautiful dog he had. Harry explained that he once was working for a doctor's wife in Clovis, New Mexico, who raised Afghan hounds. When Harry was ready to depart, she said that she was going to give him something that he could never afford: one of the Afghan puppies. She informed him that the dog was not registered, which meant that he could not sell her for a pedigree. He said when he got her, she was just a ball of fur, but within a year, she developed into what we see now. When she runs, she is "poetry in motion." She's royalty, and she knows it. She told him that an Afghan should never be named after a man: it would be like naming a dog George Washington. He said that he went to the library and found a map of Afghanistan and located the river "Amu

Darya," so he named his dog Darya. He admitted that Darya had been an asset in many ways: the way he acted, dressed, etc. He was determined not to embarrass her and managed to groom her every night.

I noticed that the lean-to made use of some of the material from the shop downstairs. I commented on his ingenuity—including his dog on the roof—but warned him that he was trespassing and that I was obligated to report it. He admitted that he had clocked the security rounds and had been careful to avoid being seen. He facetiously suggested that we needed showers in the dressing rooms. He then confided that he had used a sling to transport the dog. He didn't elaborate exactly how it was done.

We bade our "guests" adieu and I agreed not to report the incident for twenty-four hours.

12

The next day, I went to the roof to be certain that Harry Selby and Darya were gone. I really didn't know what to expect when I climbed to the roof. The area was cleared—with no signs of man or beast. Even the lean-to had been "struck" (disassembled) and I suspected the components replaced.

I had thought about the man and dog often. It would have been interesting to know more about them. I wondered what it had to do with all the other happenings this fall. I had said that our new college president didn't deserve the bizarre events: although she might not yet be aware of the "squatters on the roof" that we had never had before; a freshman' murder/suicide with the smoke tower being involved, and a possible investigation by a federal agency.

I still say that Harry Selby and Darya should be more than just an isolated incident. They should be a Greek tragedy's *deus ex machina* that would descend and solve our problems. Stay tuned!

13

As the tech crew continued constructing the scenery for *Yerma*, I couldn't help overhearing their discussions of our uninvited guests. They were impressed with Harry Selby's ingenuity in selecting the theatre roof for their abode with the possibility of descending to the theatre's loft in case of inclement weather. The crew seemed to value the brief encounter and regretted their departure. Although I agreed, I couldn't say so—for obvious reasons.

Since the false proscenium would be 40 feet wide by 20 feet high, it was decided to lay $4' \times 8'$ sheets of $1/2''$ plywood on the floor and block in the pelvic design before constructing the four inner sets. After sketching the profile, cutting and assembling the components and painting it black, we suspended the unit upstage (behind) the main house curtain. We were now ready to tackle the individual settings. At the rear of the stage, we have a huge cyclorama (or sky drop) that can be lighted with various colors plus projections of clouds, rainbows, stars, etc. to complete the *mise en scène.*

That night before rehearsal, I was downstairs in my office when the stage manager knocked on the door to inform me that a freshman had come backstage volunteering to work on *Yerma*. The freshman said that she had been off campus and missed the auditions. I was about to ask what positions were open, when the stage manager startled me with: "She said her name was Ashley Bowman!"

"Ashley Bowman?"

"That is what she said," was the reply.

After gaining a semblance of composure, I asked the stage manager to ask "Miss Bowman" to come by my office.

As I waited for my unexpected visitor, I was attempting to prepare questions that should elicit an explanation for the debacle that the campus had experienced. After 10 minutes with no response, I went to the stage to find out why the holdup. The stage manager was surprised that the student had failed to comply with my invitation. She said that she had offered to accompany her, but "Ashley" had said that she knew where my office was because of the theatre scholarship auditions held there during the summer. I was in a quandary as to what to do. Had Ashley Bowman reported her own return to the college, or were we the only ones with knowledge of her reprise? Plus the fact that we now knew nothing of her whereabouts.

I began to wonder if the stage manager actually saw "Ashley Bowman." Chances were that they had never met, since they were not members of the same class (academically, not socially). In that case, she was obliged to take the girl's word for her identity. If she were an imposter, what was her motive? If she really were Ashley Bowman, she had some explaining to do! In either case, the morrow should be interesting.

14

My approach to the next day followed my daily schedule: breakfast in the snack bar, checking my mail and teaching two theatre courses before noon. There was no reference to last night's non-visitation by student or faculty. (Usually the campus Post Office clerk helped the faculty stay abreast of the campus news and rumors.) Since there was absolutely no feed-back to last night's encounter, I actually began to wonder if I had dreamt the whole thing.

The following night's *Yerma* rehearsal was not only a carbon copy of the previous night but a reassurance of its validity. I was again in my office when the stage manager entered with "She's back!" Being somewhat surprised and disappointed that the bearer of the news had not approached me during the day to discuss last night's happening, I was obliged to ask: "Did Ashley say why she failed to come by my office last night?"

"No, only that on the way down to your office, she remembered an appointment she had, but she would be by to see you tomorrow."

I thanked her and told her to get the cast ready for Act II.

As I looked over my notes, I wondered if the next day would be a déjà vu of the previous night.

15

With no morning classes the next day, I remained in my office awaiting Ashley Bowman's arrival. I admit that I was glad that I had been forewarned not only of the visit but her presence on campus. I could understand the stage manager's response since she was an upperclassman and probably didn't either recognize her or remember the name of the missing freshman. (I didn't know how much the campus knew about the chimney discovery.) To have her appear in my office unannounced would have been like seeing an apparition!

I was about to declare the morning a lost cause when there was a knock on the door. Instead of rushing to greet her, I stood and invited her in. As she entered, she glanced around and remarked, "Just as I remembered it."

I offered her a chair and as I took my seat, remarked, "You look remarkably well for being dead for a week!"

"What do you mean?" she asked, with no trace or sarcasm.

"There is a body at the city morgue with your name tied to its toe."

As the girl looked completely baffled, I attempted to bring her up-to-date. I told her about Ashley Bowman's disappearance, the search, the inability of locating her parents or school records; the finding of a body in the old smoke chimney, and the discovery that this so-called "freshman" was 30 years old with two degrees from the University of Illinois in Champaign-Urbana.

Ashley Bowman was apparently bewildered by the aftermath of her departure, but she did attempt to explain that there were *two* Ashley Bowmans at her school—one ten years ago—but that one was a male and he attended the University of Illinois.

I asked what were her immediate plans?

She replied that she was on her way to the Registrar to check in and since she had registered for classes before "Rat," she would see if she could still get in them. I wished her the best of luck and said I would look forward to her auditioning for the next play.

As she departed, I wondered if I would ever see her again: she had a knack of disappearing.

16

At the snack bar the following morning, there was no mention of Ashley Bowman's return—not even at the Post Office. I thought perhaps that the word hadn't gotten out as of yet. I also thought that she might have disappeared again, and I began to question if it were really Ashley Bowman in my office. Of course, I was distracted by her remark, "Just as I remembered it." Could I really swear to her authenticity? She never explained who the dead person was (understandable), or how the corpse had the same physical characteristics as her Illinois namesake—except that the corpse was not a male. So now, we not only had a corpse whose cause of death was questionable, but whose identity was unknown!

It seems that the more we knew about the vanishing freshman, the more questions we asked. We were told that when Ashley was discovered missing, all of her personal effects remained in her dorm room. According to what she told the *Yerma* stage manager, she had to leave campus that night without telling anyone. The question arose; how was she able to depart without her personal effects? I have not heard whether she returned to her dorm as yet. In fact, I'm not even sure that she is still on campus.

Since Ashley Bowman was alive and supposedly back on campus (at least as witnessed by the stage manager and myself) it would seem that a concerted effort would be made to identify the body now in the city morgue. In so doing, perhaps her *raison d'être* would also be established. (I would like to think that all of this has been going on while I was out of the loop and second-guessing.)

17

A day or so later, I went over to the campus security office to speak with Jason Cabot concerning the identity of the body in the city morgue. He said that the coroner and the police supposed it was the missing Ashley Bowman. However, since Miss Bowman had returned to the campus the police looked through the file of missing persons and found a young woman of the right age—same height, weight and color of hair. They notified the authorities and are waiting on fingerprints, dental records and her supposed DNA.

I thanked Jason for the information and added that now we might also be able to learn why she was on campus.

After I left, it occurred to me that he hadn't said where she was from. Not that it would make any difference—except perhaps to mend my curiosity.

On the way back to my office, I detoured by the chimney tower behind the physical plant. The NO TRESPASSING sign had been taken down and the cordon tape around the tower base had been removed. Not that I was expecting to find anything, but I walked around the chimney anyway. Finding nothing, I looked inside the chimney: The floor of the base showed no signs of the supposed impact of a body falling 17 stories. The maintenance crew had no doubt scrubbed the floor. I did see the metal ladder attached to the inner wall of the chimney. There was no landing near the top—not that I thought there should be one.

Anyway, over the weekend, I decided that I had contributed enough time and energy to something that was not really my bailiwick anyway.

18

I attempted to focus my attention on the direction and the technical aspects of *Yerma*. The costumer, Diana Douglas, was busy measuring, building, and ordering the 28-plus costumes. Although there are only 28 characters in the play, scenes take place at different times and locations, therefore some of the characters require more than one costume.

The third member of the Theatre Department, our only Ph.D., whom we refer to as our "colleague of letters," teaches the literature courses and is responsible for the printed play bills, programs and publicity. When a play is in rehearsal, we are all busy wearing our "many hats" (both academic and production).

As well as one strongly attempts to ignore the past, it has a way of catching up with you. This interruption had to do with Ashley Bowman, the returning freshman who had been missing. One of the faculty-student committees that had to do with student discipline, had Ashley Bowman on the carpet for leaving campus during "Rat" week without permission and precipitating a campus-wide search for a missing student. I was the only faculty member who had contact with Ashley Bowman prior to registration, so I was interviewed independently before the committee. I told them that I had auditioned the girl for a Theatre Talent Award during the summer and had recommended her for the award. I told them I had met with Ashley only once since then and had learned nothing as to why she left campus. I was then told the reason she had given for leaving, with the stipulation that it was strictly hush-hush. Ashley Bowman had left to have an abortion!

I responded that she surely knew that she was pregnant before coming on campus and that it would have been better to have had the procedure before registration—unless she was keeping it from her parents. When I didn't get a response from the committee (what did I know about those things), I recommended that she be put on some sort of probation, rather than expelled. I was thanked and returned to my domicile.

I had no more than concluded that distraction when there was news from the Camon Police concerning the body in the morgue found in the college smoke tower. The fingerprints, dental records and DNA had now arrived.

I don't know how long it takes to compare these vital statistics, but I think that it would have been better to have waited for the tests. (I suppose that a bit of news was considered good PR for the department.)

19

I was told by Jason Cabot that the vital statistics of the missing person matched those of the body now in the city morgue which had been discovered in the base of the smoke tower. She had now been identified as Marsha Keys of Watkinsville, GA, a town south of Athens, on Routes US 129 & 441. Her parents had informed campus security that Marsha owned a car which security had located by checking the license plates from Oconee County. It turned out to be a van with an array of research and notebooks that revealed her interest in Nunnery College and the smoke tower in particular. She had apparently chosen the fall opening because with all the new students, she wouldn't be noticed.

It is amazing how an urban legend can become not only truly believed, but can become one's purpose in life. It happened in the '30s, when the college was moving to a new location. A smoke tower was to be erected and steam tunnels dug as the dormitories and other campus buildings were being built. It was during this time that a backhoe operator made a discovery that potentially could prove as nefarious as Pandora's Box. Covering it with a tarpaulin, his mistake was reporting his find to his supervisor (builder-contractor). The on-the-spot examination determined that it should be "relocated." Rather than being rewarded for his discovery, the worker suffered the misfortune of his body becoming part of the concrete footing for the 170-foot smoke tower!

I had heard this story when I first joined the faculty at Nunnery, as Miss Keys also probably had when she was a child. It was more personal to her because the backhoe operator was her grandfather! As she grew up, she became obsessed by the legend and was determined to research and to "right" it. According to her notebook, she interviewed relatives of her grandfather and of his co-workers. They claimed that the trove contained records of the mulatto breeding farm that the Nunnery Plantation ran supplying brothels throughout the area before the war. Finally she decided upon her retaliation.

Apparently Marsha Keys had a strong dislike for the smoke tower—for obvious reasons. So her priority was to have it removed. She didn't spell out her plan, but her demise at the base of the structure might accomplish it. Then it dawned on me: the plunge was intentional—suicide was the plan!

20

I don't know how Ashley Bowman's classmates acted (or reacted) when she returned to campus. It was not like they had known her any length of time; everyone was a stranger when the semester started. Other than her roommates, there wasn't much of a chance of establishing any sort of a rapport, especially since she probably had planned to leave campus when Rat was over that Saturday night. However, since she possessed no transportation, she most likely had made arrangements for an accomplice to meet her and drive her to her destination. Of course, on the other hand, there was no proof that she had ever been pregnant or, that she had left campus for an abortion.

I had heard nothing about any plans to demolish the smoke tower. Upon discovering the body in the well of the tower, it occurred to me that the college might remove the obsolete structure so that it wouldn't be a reminder of the tragedy. Whether it was murder or suicide, the site would have been a 170–foot blight on the campus. I wouldn't think even a planned suicide for that purpose would alter the perception of the event.

Marsha Keys' family came to the campus and claimed possession of her van. If her body had had any identification or artifacts, the mistaken identity would have been avoided. However, the lawsuit wouldn't: the family was suing the college for not sealing the smoke tower in order to prevent incidents such as the one that claimed the life of their daughter. I wondered how she knew so much about the chimney that prompted her to decide to plunge to her death. She obviously had been on campus earlier, to have discovered the inside ladder to the top. (I had ruled out the "human fly" syndrome possibility.) One wonders what would have been her plan had the smoke tower been sealed!

21

The afternoon of the second week of *Yerma* rehearsals, I received word that Amy Thorp, the student playing Yerma, had been taken sick and was in the infirmary. The stage manager reminded me that we hadn't selected any understudies. I asked her had Ashley Bowman been around? She said that she had, in fact, and was a "ninja" (our jargon name for a member of the backstage crew). I told her that Ashley had read for the part in the talent award audition during the summer and should be able to step in. The stage manager agreed and would get in touch with her. If only all problems could be handled as easily . . .

I hadn't been able to find out the nature of the illness that had put our lead actress in the infirmary, or how long the doctors estimated confinement. From all reports as well as my own observations at rehearsals, Ashley was an excellent choice for the understudy. She had gotten the blocking (where and how to move) from the stage manager and had already memorized most of the lines. If she should have to play the role, the rented costumes would fit! My only concern had to do with her emotional reaction to the theme of the play in light of her recent abortion.

During the week, word from the infirmary wasn't encouraging: Amy Thorp, the student who was to play *Yerma,* was not doing well. It was thought that she had some sort of stomach virus, but was not responding to medication. Then later, they thought that she might have ingested some sort of poison. How could that have happened? A person is not poisoned unless she does it to herself or it is given to her.

What kind of poison? I understand that an allergy to food such as peanuts or seafood can be deadly to some, but it's inconceivable that anything so drastic could be perpetrated on a college campus! True, there are examples of this in professional theatre where a person's career might be at stake. In theatre history, I recall that an early eighteenth-century French actress, the beautiful Adrienne Lecouvreur (1692–1730), was poisoned at the height of her fame by a rival. Her tragic death had inspired both poets and playwrights.

However, Ashley Bowman had no assurance that she would be selected as the understudy—or did she?

22

The Keys family took Marsha's body back to Watkinsville for the burial. I don't think anyone from the college attended the funeral. In fact, no one knew her except as a corpse and the cause of the lawsuit against the college. I don't know why it had taken Marsha so long to come to Nunnery to inspect the site, since it had been over sixty years since the event—that is, if it ever took place: Her missing grandfather might have spent the rest of his life on some South Pacific island! In fact, I heard that the trove that was discovered is now in the Nunnery Room of our library. Apparently our philanthropist wasn't as ashamed of the mulatto breeding business as first thought (or as everyone thought).

I hadn't heard anything of the college's response to the suicide or the lawsuit. I would think that the removal of the smoke tower might be considered for the sake of public relations, but it wouldn't affect the lawsuit since its concern was the access to the tower's interior. I thought that the defense should concentrate on the demeanor of Marsha Keys, the victim. Investigation might suggest that she was not totally rational—being obsessed with the urban legend that her grandfather became part of the foundation of the smoke tower because of his discovery.

I had a welcome surprise at our afternoon crew session. A couple of the girls were relating their experience of seeing Harry Selby and Darya at the city park. They said that Harry and his dog were attracting quite a bit of attention. I asked if they had spoken to him. They said that they had, and that he remembered them. I asked how did he look? They replied that he and Darya looked O.K. and that Harry had asked about me. He also said that he and Darya would pay us a visit before leaving town. I thanked them for the message. (I didn't say "warning" because I actually would be glad to see them again!)

23

Better news from the infirmary today. Amy Thorp, the *Yerma* leading lady, was improving, but was so weak from the ordeal that she was being sent home to recuperate. They still weren't sure of the cause, but she was responding to treatment. Since there was no prognosis as to the length of confinement, we decided to make the change in the cast permanent; Ashley Bowman was now playing Yerma.

I don't know why, but the transition seemed too easy. True, it was partially my fault. It was I who asked about Ashley, who had appeared back stage when she returned to campus. I've often heard the expression that there is always "someone waiting in the wings."

In spite of my apprehension, rehearsals for *Yerma* were going well. The cast accepted Ashley in the title role. In fact, the whole play seemed to take on new life. My initial evaluation of Ashley Bowman was right: She was *good!*

Not only was the play taking shape on stage, but the scenery was on schedule. All the costumes had been fitted, the publicity distributed and the playbills were at the printer's. I was feeling rather smug when I saw Harry Selby coming down the aisle of the theater that afternoon. I left the stage to meet him. The crew saw me leave and followed when they saw the visitors. As they converged on Darya, Harry recognized the two students he had met in the park and acknowledged them.

As he surveyed the stage, the false proscenium attracted his attention. "I feel that I'm in an anatomy class."

"Thank you," was my response. "I was attempting to suggest the theme of Lorca's *Yerma.*"

"I know the play but I never thought about the theme so graphically."

"It was about the only chance I had to use symbolism," I replied. "All the other scenery was just standard stage-craft."

"I didn't say it was bad," Harry replied. "In fact, I think it is rather innovative."

Since I didn't wish to pursue the subject, I changed it with "What are you doing here in Camon?"

He said that he had been in Atlanta, but had been back in Camon for a week.

"Where are you staying?"

"You mean, where are we sleeping?" he replied. "Under the overpass down at the Interstate. It hasn't been too bad so far."

"How do you travel—with your dog?" I asked.

"Not by bus or train, of course, but you'd be surprised how Darya gets me rides. I don't even have to use my thumb, most of the time. She is my first-class ticket," he said as he stroked her affectionately.

I became more impressed by this man the more that I knew of him. I kept feeling that he was an omen of some sort—if I could only interpret it.

24

After an hour or so, Harry Selby and Darya bade us adieu and we returned to the stage. I couldn't help but think that they were a perfect example of a symbiotic relationship. He provided the food, grooming and love; she provided class, companionship and protection. Afghan hounds are not usually considered aggressive, but I understand that they were originally used to hunt leopards because of their great speed. I'm certain that when they caught a leopard, they didn't befriend it. In one of Donald Hamilton's *Matt Helm* novels, Afghans were used as guard dogs and could be quite vicious. I recall that when I first met Harry on the roof of the theatre building he said that he tried to dress and act so that Darya would not be ashamed of him. (That practice could save a lot of marriages.)

That was the last time that I saw the erudite vagabond, but a couple of days later, I received a letter from him. The address was not exactly correct, but it was precise enough that I received it. It was written on lined paper—legibly.

Dear Professor McAmby,

When you receive this letter, we will be gone, but I want to share an observation with you.

The night that Darya and I came to campus to seek our residence atop the theatre, we passed the Physical Plant, and I noticed a panel truck parked in back beside the smoke tower with a U.S. Park Service logo on the side. There was activity around the base of the tower. We waited until the truck, with two or three men, left, and then went to see what they were doing inside the tower. With my Mag Lite I could see the mutilated body of a female positioned as if she had fallen from the top of the smoke tower. I also could

48

see the inside ladder that could have provided the means to reach the top, but I think that the body was placed there. I'm writing this because I understand that the victim was first thought to be the missing student until the girl returned. The body was the identified as a deranged girl from Watkinsville whose family is suing the college for not sealing the tower, but I still think that she was placed there.

Darya and I continued our trek to the theatre in the Fine Arts Building. Since it's a professional secret, I can't tell you how we got in.

Thanks for your hospitality,
Harry Selby and friend

25

After Harry and Darya left the roof of the theatre, I said that it shouldn't be an isolated incident—that they might even prove to be a *deus ex machina*. This letter bears that out! While not exactly a classical example, it could be a contemporary equivalent. Harry's discovery could save the college a great deal of money if the charges ever went to court.

I couldn't help but reflect on Harry's conclusion(s). I could understand why Marsha Keys vetoed climbing to the top of the 170–foot tower. Our grid is 50′ above the stage, and a 50′ climb on a vertical ladder is an ordeal. Imagine a ladder almost four times as high!

Where would she find a structure approximately the same height? There used to be a water tower in the middle of Watkinsville, but the last time I went through the town, it had been removed. I remembered that water tower well: In June several years ago, I was driving my family to the Great Smokies. As we reached the south end of Watkinsville, the car radio was tuned to Athens and it announced that seven tornados were converging on Watkinsville. TAKE COVER IMMEDIATELY! We were in the middle of town by then and could see people rushing into the city hall or the courthouse. I parked and the family joined the plight. As I entered, I noticed the city's water tower was right across the street: we were entering perhaps the most dangerous building in town! Anyway, a two-hour vigil brought no tornados and no deluge of city water. Athens was not so lucky. The state troopers were on duty but it took us almost an hour to detour our way through town.

Then I remembered the logo on the truck that Harry had seen. There are government forests along the highway, and I remembered seeing a fire tower in the distance. Usually fire towers are placed on hills or knolls, but when none are available, the fire towers are higher—perhaps as high as 170 feet, with steps! To match the surface of our smoke tower's base, it too would be mounted on a cement slab. Heavy plastic would be employed to protect the surface from a suicide, and to wrap the body for removal. If a body fell 170 feet onto cement, there would have to be flecks of that cement embedded in the body. Sand should be sprinkled over the plastic before the victim falls.

Obviously, I am assuming that the subject is willing: otherwise it would be murder!

26

Another clue that suggested the fire tower was the truck that was seen at the rear of the physical plant. Not only could it have been used to transport the body, but the park crew could have been members of the Keys family employed by the Park Service.

So much for conjecture. I had never seen the body of a person killed by falling, so I was obviously out of my element. However, since Harry Selby had selected me as a confidant, I was attempting to make sense out of his epistle.

Ignoring the peripheral matters and back to what I was employed to do. I just hope that the members of the Thomebeh Society will see the play. True, the Society built the arena theatre across the lake for us, but I would like to show them that some plays almost demand a proscenium stage—especially a multiple set show such as *Yerma*. And of course, the use of a symbolic inner proscenium would be impossible in the arena.

The dress rehearsal for *Yerma* went very well and our final dress rehearsal was tonight. I was a bit apprehensive about my inner proscenium perhaps being too graphic, especially after Harry Selby's remark that it was like being in an anatomy lab. However, it was just a silhouette of the pelvis framing the stage. I was certain half the audience wouldn't notice it, and if they did, wouldn't catch the symbolism. As I've said before, it is still an interesting design!

Opening night went well, a carbon copy of the final

dress rehearsal. It's a theatre superstition that if the final dress goes badly, opening night will be a success. I think it is just "wishful thinking." Personally, I'd take my chances on a "final dress" going well!

We had an audience of around 350. That is good for a play, although it looks sparse in our auditorium of 1100 seats. That was one reason that the Thomebeh Society had thought we should have a more intimate theatre, and built the arena theatre for us. Most of the Society was in the audience. I hadn't checked the reservations since I have finally "delegated" that chore to students, but several members of the Society congratulated me during intermission. After the play, I was really surprised to be introduced to Mr. and Mrs. Charles Bowman—by their daughter, Ashley! They thanked me for taking care of Ashley and for casting her in the play. They remembered her liking the play when she had auditioned for a Talent Award last summer. When I asked them where were they from, they replied Augusta, but that they had been out of town all fall. Originally, they were from Champaign, Illinois.

When they left, it was obvious that they had no idea that Ashley had been missing and for a while thought to be the victim of suicide—let alone her undergoing an abortion!

I would have talked with Ashley, but I was severely handicapped by being sworn to secrecy about her operation. Without a clear agenda, I told the stage manager to ask Ashley to come by my office the next day.

Ashley came by just before lunch. I asked her to have a seat and began by complimenting her on her performance. I told her that I was glad that her parents were able to attend the play's opening and that it was a pleasure to finally meet them. She thanked me and expressed her appreciation for a chance to be in *Yerma*.

I then got to the crux of the matter. "From my conversation with your parents, they apparently know nothing about your disappearance this fall and the body in the smoke tower that was initially thought to be yours."

All she could say was, "I know."

"Don't you think that they have the right to know?" I continued, still avoiding the "secret."

Ashley hesitated, thought a moment before responding: "Yes, I suppose so, but I didn't want them to worry."

"But they will find out eventually, and it would be better if you told them."

"Will I have to tell them why?" she asked.

"That is up to you, but it is better to tell them the truth rather than to lie," I advised.

She said that she would tell them the first chance he got and then thanked me for my counsel as she left.

I don't think that my handling of the session would win any award, but at least I didn't jeopardize the committee's integrity.

27

Yerma's run was successful. We got a good review in the local paper with no mention of the "suggestive proscenium" and attendance was better than average. The following week we were busy striking (dismantling and storing) the scenery. Our second production was to be in the arena theatre across the lake with little or no scenery.

Our costumer had chosen Emlyn Williams' *Night Must Fall* as her play. This melodrama by the British playwright has been a popular play for amateur theatre groups for a generation. The psychopath in the drama, who carries around a severed head (presumably) in a hat box, was originally played by the playwright himself. I had directed the play several years ago in Portales, New Mexico, at Eastern New Mexico University. In our summer program, we had as our guest performer Mr. Walter Abel, the distinguished Broadway and Hollywood actor to star in the popular French play *The Enchanted*. Since I was to direct *Night Must Fall* next, I asked Mr. Abel if he would record the judge's instructions to the unseen jury in the prologue. He obliged and I still have the tape with his famous baritone voice that will be used in our production. In the arena, because of the audience's proximity to the stage, one has to be concerned with violence. Fortunately, the most violent scene is the psychopath suffocating an old woman in a wheelchair with a pillow as the lights go down in Act II. (Not nearly as gruesome as the eye gouging scene in Shakespeare's *King Lear.*)

Auditions for *Night Must Fall* are scheduled for next week. I understand that they will be held in the auditorium rather than in the Thomebeh Arena Theatre. The auditorium is in the center of the campus, making it more accessible. I don't know how many from *Yerma* are planning to read for the parts. Theatre majors and other interested students want to participate as much as possible, but rehearsals are time-consuming and I don't know if the men in the *Yerma* cast are interested in doing another play so soon. Perhaps the director, Diana Douglas, had already contacted some potential talent. The role of Danny, the baby-faced psychotic killer, would be the most demanding. The other men are rather stock characters. (The playwright understandably wanted to be the star at its premiere.)

We had done plays in the Thomebeh Arena Theatre before. I had not directed my plays there, but had assisted the other two directors in staging theirs. The theatre's design is a replica of the Thomebeh's mosque-like headquarters on the outskirts of Camon. It seats 200-plus, on four tiers surrounding a 26′ stage. There is a hydraulic lift center stage. So far, we have only used it to bring props and furniture stored in the basement, but it could be used for special effects if needed. The lighting is state-of-the-art that can be focused and controlled remotely. The theatre also provides dressing, make-up and restrooms at the rear of the building. One can understand that while we didn't particularly want an arena theatre, this offer was too good to be refused.

28

Since I hadn't heard anything about the suit that the Keys family was bringing against the college for not sealing the smoke tower and thus preventing their daughter's death, I became concerned about my role in thwarting the charge. Of course, I do have Harry Selby's letter describing what he and Darya saw that night, but since he and his dog are long gone, it could have been written by anyone. However, the more I thought about it, I think that Harry was correct—that is, Marsha Keys fell from some place other than the Nunnery College smoke tower. I still plan to show the letter to Jason Cabot. However, he probably had already considered the possibility.

From a layman's perspective, *if* the parents really thought that their daughter climbed to the top of the chimney on her own power, and then jumped, and *if* it could be proven that such an act was impossible, then the case would be dismissed. If however, it could be proven that the parents were aware of the alternate site and were blaming the college for providing the smoke tower as the crime site, then charges could be brought against them for fraud . . . and the men in the government truck could be indicted for perpetuating the fraud if it were consensual—for murder if it were not.

When I finally found time to go to the campus security office, I was able to catch Jason there. He said that he had questioned the possibility of the victim climbing a 170-foot ladder. He said that when they refurbished the chimney, they decided against the interior ladder in favor of extension ladders on the outside. All they had to do was to guide hooks over the rim to support the scaffolding.

I then showed him Harry Selby's letter which he read, Xeroxed and returned with his "thank you" and added that it could be "live ammunition" if the Keys family were foolish enough to pursue their lawsuit.

29

I hadn't seen Ashley Bowman since our little get-together after *Yerma*. I understood that she hadn't auditioned for the arena play, and since she wasn't registered for any theatre courses, I didn't even know if she was still on campus. That is, until she appeared on stage one afternoon when the tech crew was busy sorting hardware. She knew most of the crew since most of them had also been involved in *Yerma*. As she was preparing to leave, she approached me and asked if she could see me the following morning. We agreed on a time and she left through the auditorium. (Apparently the elusive Miss Bowman was still on campus!)

At the agreed-on time, Ashley arrived. So far, so good.

"What's on your mind?" was my inspired opener.

"A couple of things," she replied seriously.

Before I could say anything, she continued with, "First, I don't know what that committee told you, but I did not have an abortion when I was off-campus in September: I just told them that because they wouldn't believe what really happened."

I didn't reply.

"I had just entered my dorm room after the 'Rat' ceremony that Saturday night when I was abducted!"

"Where were your roommates or suite mates at the time?" was all I could come up with.

"I don't know—I was alone!"

"Who were your abductors—how many were there?"

"That's just it: that's why I didn't tell what really happened."

"Are you able to tell me now?" I asked.

"I'll try, but I warn you, it's hard to believe." Ashley paused, as if to gather her thoughts.

She continued. "Suddenly, the room was filled with a blinding bright light and I guess I fainted. When I came to, I was alone in a strange room."

"Were you on any kind of medication that day?" I inquired.

"Nothing! Not even an aspirin."

"Why did you think that you were abducted? After you fainted, you could have been taken to the infirmary or to a hospital. Either would have been strange to you."

"It's what happened next," she continued. "A strange little creature appeared and spoke to me."

I wasn't buying this.

"It could have been a hallucination reminiscent of Steven Spielberg's *Close Encounters of the Third Kind* with Richard Dreyfuss? Although it came out in 1977 you have probably seen a video of it," I suggested.

"I've seen the film," she admitted, "but this creature was telling me what to do."

O.K., I thought. Now we have a combination of *Close Encounters* and *Joan of Arcadia.* True the TV series didn't begin until after classes had started, but there had been extensive promos during the summer of "Joan" speaking with "God."

Then I had to ask, "What did it tell you to do?"

"It told me to audition for *Yerma,*" she replied. "I explained that I was missing auditions." But the creature said, "Just do it!"

"That's why I came to the theatre when I got back on campus," she continued, "and volunteered to be a ninja, or whatever it is called."

A horrible thought crossed my mind: did her "hallucination" have something to do with the affliction of the actress playing Yerma, or was Ashley involved? Or none of the above?

Without delving into that aspect of the "abduction," I asked her how long she was kept hostage.

She replied that she lost track of time, but when she got back, it must have been over a week.

I then asked her if she had any idea of where she was kept?

Since she didn't know Camon, she had no idea.

"Well then, how did you get back?"

'The same way that I was abducted," she replied, "only this time I was given an injection and I woke up back in my room."

"You keep using the word 'abducted,' but you only mention one 'creature.' Just how many were there?" I finally asked.

"There were several, but what was strange, they didn't come in through the door: they would just appear!" she replied and then added, "I'm not certain that the room even had a door."

After a short interval, I suggested that she let her explanation to the committee stand and whatever she had told her classmates, adapt that to tell her parents.

I wasn't proud of my advice, but it might keep her off the psychiatric couch for the time being!

30

The session with Ashley Bowman was disturbing. On the surface, it was a fanciful escapade: nothing could be verified. Her abduction had been accomplished when she had fainted; her return concealed by a knockout drug. The place of her imprisonment was vague and the description of her abductors imaginative. Her motive for altering her story in light of its absurdity? Unknown—*unless it happened to be true!*

We have come to expect every school year to be the same old, same old. I suspect if we didn't, we would become apprehensive and eventually look for a different kind of employment. We are geared to handle the unexpected, but when we are plagued by the unexpected, as happened this fall, we attempt to solve it as quickly as possible in order to return to the status quo. There are committees and designated persons to oversee the effort. So far, the academic area seems to be coping, and so are the students. The missing student has returned, and the leading actress in *Yerma* was the victim of a mysterious illness and had to be replaced by an understudy. The body in the smoke tower was identified as a suicide victim from Watkinsville whose family is suing the college for not sealing the tower.

It has been a fall to be remembered!

31

The next week, we received some really bad news: Amy Tharp, the actress originally cast as Yerma, who was taken sick and eventually sent home, *had died.* According to her parents, she was recuperating nicely, but last weekend, she had a seizure that proved to be fatal. An autopsy was being performed to determine the exact cause of her death. It sounded to me remarkably similar to the seizure that caused the death of the popular sitcom star John Ritter last fall, apparently caused by an artery erupting in his chest. There was no warning, and nothing could be done.

All of us in the theatre were concerned because Amy was taken ill after a rehearsal of the play. We suspected that there would be an investigation depending on what the autopsy revealed. We were all cognizant of the diagnosis that poison might have been involved. If that was proven to be correct, it was going to be an ordeal to even approaching the status quo.

Fortunately, as far as I knew, I was the only person who was aware of Ashley Bowman's alternate version of her absence from the college. The "extra-terrestrial" slant might not only reflect on her bearing but might introduce or suggest the presence of some "celestial potion."

The following week, the dreaded result of the autopsy became evident by the arrival of a cadre of investigators from some government agency. The entire cast and crew from *Yerma* were interrogated, as well as the theatre and infirmary staffs. I don't know which version of her absence Ashley used. If a polygraph had been employed, it would be interesting to know the result of either story!

After a week, the college received the results of the inquiry. The cause of death had been the seizure. Apparently it had nothing to do with her initial illness, which was caused by a stomach virus. Since the report did not identify the virus or its source (if either was even known) Ashley's extra-terrestrial rendezvous perhaps shouldn't be totally discounted!

32

A day or so later, I received an e-mail from Ashley Bow-man. I don't mind sending e-mail if necessary (my student secretary handles that for me) but I don't like receiving them. However, this one was interesting because it had to do with her "abduction."

Dear Sir:

(The title was given years ago by a student who had just seen Sidney Poitier in *To Sir with Love.*)
I've often been asked if I liked the title, I would reply, "it's better than 'Hey, you!' "

I was at the Thomebeh Arena Theatre last night watch-ing the rehearsal for *Night Must Fall.* It was strange because the interior was exactly like the room I was kept in by my abductors except there were no tiers of seats.

Damn, I thought. *She was in the headquarters of the Thomebeh Society's dome structure!* (I apologize for the ex-pletive. I feel like David O. Selznick filming *Gone with the Wind:* There was no other word that would convey the same response.)
Then it hit me: What possible connection did the ab-duction have with the Thomebeh Society? It would pro-vide credence to the supernatural aspect of the trek, but it still doesn't explain the Society's involvement. I would bet that Ashley wasn't even aware of the Thomebeh Society, let alone the similarity of its headquarters to our arena theatre. "Grasping for straws" might best explain this reminis-

cence. I still wondered which version Ashley Bowman used at the inquiry.

I pretty much had put Ashley's alternate version behind me until something more valid would present itself—one way or the other. And that happened a week or so later: I received a note from Ms. Celia Hemphill, the attorney for the Thomebeh Society.

Dear Professor McAmby:
    The Society is pleased that your second play will be presented in The Thomebeh Arena Theatre. The Society enjoyed your production of Lorca's *Yerma,* especially the performance of Miss Bowman in the title role. The young lady displayed much talent. The Society was happy to provide facilities for her during her acclimation to Nunnery College life in the fall.

                    Cordially,
                    Celia H. Hemphill

Well, I wanted validity—so I received it. It said nothing about the "alliance," but apparently I would have to reconcile myself to the fact at least part of Ashley's atlernate version was true!

33

I don't know why, but I seem to have a feeling of responsibility regarding the smoke tower debacle. I suppose it has to do with the fact that the victim was first thought to be the missing freshman whom I interviewed for a Theatre Talent Award during the summer. However, I hadn't seen her since then and I certainly didn't discover her in the chimney. In fact, because of the cordon, I didn't even see the site until the body had been removed and identified. The only association I had with the tragedy was receiving a letter from Harry Selby describing what he thought to be the dead body having been placed inside the tower at night. I, in turn, delivered the letter to the head of campus security. If the victim's family decides to pursue their charging the college with negligence for not sealing off the smoke tower, that letter with its ramification should squelch their ridiculous suit.

I couldn't help but wonder about Harry Selby and Darya when he introduced himself to me atop the theatre building last fall. I, of course, recognized that Harry Selby was a pseudonym. According to Bernard Sobel's *Theatre Handbook,* "George Spelvin" is the traditional pseudonym for an actor playing two or more roles or who wanted his identity shielded from the audience. The auditor added that there was another pseudonym used by actors: Harry Selby. I was impressed with his honesty as well as his other traits.

He may not have been a classical *deus ex machina,* but his role was nevertheless important!

34

My attention turned to the Thomebeh Arena Theatre. Originally the plans called for four tiers, 36″ wide and 12″ high. I immediately questioned the four entrances (N, S, E, W) since there are no doors in the theatre-in-the-round, and the actors would have to time their entrances from the sides of the auditorium and come down steps to the stage. So now the four tiers would be only 6″ high, and instead of steps, there are four 12′ long ramps, 2′ high and 4′ wide. This change in the plans seemed to provide safer entrances and exits to the stage—for both the actors and audience.

Since this was the first time Diana Douglas had directed in the arena theatre, I asked her how everything was working out to which she replied, "fine," that she was pleased with her cast, and especially with the young fellow playing Danny, the psychopath.

Diana also said that Ashley Bowman had approached her asking if she could do lights for the show. Since Diana hadn't yet assigned anyone, she had said it was O.K., if I agreed. Regardless of who was assigned as lighting director, I would have to train that person because of our new state-of-the-art control system, so I had no problem there. Personally, I was pleased to work with Ashley again. If she proved to be as good a technician as an actress, we were in luck!

I asked Diana if there were any special lighting requirements? She replied just one: when the old lady is being smothered with the pillow, there has to be a fast dim-out in order for wheelchair and victim to leave via the south exit before the intermission lights come up.

I told her that we should be able to handle that—and

that I assumed "Danny" would wheel her out during the blackout.

She replied that she hoped that he could "break character" enough to do it.

What was disturbing was that she had her doubts . . .

I sent word to Ashley to come by my office to work out a schedule for instruction in the operation of the arena theatre's new lighting facilities. I assumed that she would be familiar with the computerized console, so most of the instruction would have to do with the remote control of focusing and the changing of filters since each instrument had a stock of colors that could be changed at will. (The only time an instrument would be handled manually would be to replace a lamp.) The control of an instrument's "on-and-off" as well as its dimming had been accomplished by remote control since electricity had come to the theatre. It was being able to remotely control the focus and the color changing that really impressed us!

Ashley and I got together later that week at the arena theatre's light and sound booth at the south end of the theatre, above the dressing rooms. I checked her out on the console and explained the remote system of focusing and changing filters. She asked where were the instruments, since she couldn't see them?

I explained that they were recessed in slots in the oval walls so that they would be accessible from the corridors surrounding the auditorium. After dimming the house chandelier, Ashley practiced changing the focus and filters on several instruments. She too was impressed.

Then she asked if there was a light plot? I told her that I didn't think so—just general illumination on the entire stage. First, cross-light each N.S.E.W. area with 2 Fresnels each; then cross-light between: NS EW, NW with 2 Fresnels each. In your cross lighting, use warm and cool color in each instrument. You now have individual control of all six areas. (There are many warm and cool colors but certain combinations work better together.) There are no specials. The only quick dim-out is when the psychopath is smothering the old lady. It has to be fast in order for the victim and wheelchair to be off stage when the intermission lights come up. (We turned on 12 unfocused Fresnels for a practice cue before bringing up the house lights.) Perfect!

Before leaving the control room, I couldn't pass up the opportunity to share my letter from the Thomebeh Society's attorney, Celia Hemphill, with Ashley Bowman.

"I think that you might be interested in a letter I received last week," I began. "It was from Celia Hemphill, she's the attorney for the Thomebeh Society."

No response.

"It is the organization that built this arena theatre for us."

With still no semblance of response, I delivered the Society's message. "The Society said that they enjoyed our production of *Yerma*—especially your performance in the title role—that you displayed much talent and that the society was happy to provide facilities for you during your acclimation to college life in the fall."

"Does this mean that you now believe that I was really abducted?" she asked.

"It seems that you were at the Thomebeh headquarters," I replied carefully. "How you got there, and the extra-terrestrial element, is questionable."

"I told you all that I remember," she said. "I'm sorry."

My reply was, "For what it is worth, I'm just glad that you didn't have an abortion. Let's leave it at that." We left the theatre.

35

When I directed *Night Must Fall* in New Mexico, it was a summer production—in a tent. Come to think of it, it too was an "arena" production with the audience surrounding the stage. It would be great to do that play again and have the curtain come down when Danny was smothering the old lady rather than having the scene "struck" in a blackout.

Of course, in a "tent" production the audience expects to "see" scene changes; Diana confessed that she was having her Danny "strike" the chair so that he would have to stop the smothering. (The reader shouldn't be too surprised that often an actor becomes overly absorbed in a role, especially that of a neurotic/psychotic nature; in fact, that type of role often attracts a similar type of individual.) Diana says that the leather hat box "Danny" clutches, supposedly containing a severed head, never leaves him—he even takes it home with him. The cast say that they wouldn't even dare look in it!

I have heard that in the '50s a well-known British actor (perhaps Ronald Colman?) was starring in Shakespeare's *Othello* and become so consumed by the role that one night he "actually" choked Desdemona. (We will monitor our method actor!)

I met with Ashley later to set lights in the arena theatre. Normally that is a chore involving one person in the control booth and another on a ladder adjusting and focusing the instruments on different areas on the stage, and changing colors according to instructions given by the lighting director in the booth. However, in this theatre, all these options can be accomplished remotely from the control booth. With my assistance, Ashley focused the twelve Fresnels on the 6 acting areas as instructed. Since each area was cross-lighted by 2 instruments, she had to select a warm color and a cool color for each area.

As I have mentioned, there are many combinations available and experience teaches one what combinations to use for different effects. Ashley had chosen R33 No Color Pink and R54 Special Lavender for her color combination. Since there were no "specials," she was able to use the same combination for all 12 Freshnels. If only we could "program" actors as we have accomplished in the technical field!

36

I happened to run into Yancy Doogal, the actor playing Danny in Diana's *Night Must Fall*. I asked him to follow me to one of the dressing rooms backstage. He said of course and did so.

When we arrived and found chairs, I told him that I was happy to inform him that the director was impressed with his Danny in the play.

He thanked me and said that he was enjoying playing the role.

I then said that the cast was somewhat uncomfortable because he was allowing the character to dominate him—like taking the hat box home with him.

Yancy said, not to worry, because that was part of his plan. He admitted that perhaps he should have cleared this with the director, but the play depends upon the other characters mistrusting and fearing him. If they really did feel this way, it should project to the audience. If it was too much, he'd talk with the director to tone it down some. "Incidentally," he added, "I put the hat box in my car every night—just for the effect."

I told him that I was glad that he was in control but to be sure to confide in the director, as she was concerned about him "breaking character" in time to strike the chair. He told me to assure her that he would!

I spoke to Diana a couple of days later about my conversation with Yancy. She thanked me and said she had noticed the change—and that he had talked with her.

Tech rehearsal was scheduled for the next week and everything seemed ready. You might be surprised that I didn't read the riot act to Yancy concerning his "extension of character." I might have—if I hadn't had a similar experience years ago when I was directing Eugene O'Neill's *Desire Under the Elms*. The actor playing Cabot, the father, was such a despicable person that I thought several times about replacing him. One day, I spoke to him about it. He explained that he was supposed to be hated by his three sons and his new wife: he was just making it easier for them. Anyway, it worked that time!

37

I thought that I had seen and heard the last of Harry Selby and friend when they had supposedly left town after I received his letter reporting what they had witnessed on the night that they had sought refuge on our campus. Since he was a vagabond by nature (par excellence, I might add) and with Darya as his first-class ticket for transportation, I had no idea where he might be headed. I often wondered if he even had a destination. Perhaps he would let fate select his next abode?

However, this preconceived appraisal suffered a setback with the newspaper account of a man and his dog rescuing a family in Alabama. According to the article, the man and his Afghan hound were hitchhiking on US 80 in Alabama when they were offered a ride by a family of a husband, wife and an 8-year-old daughter headed west. The daughter was in the back seat but soon made friends with Darya, the dog, and its owner when they joined her. In the next two hours, they all became acquainted when they parked in a rest stop. The passenger, who identified himself as Harry Selby, took the Afghan for a walk while the mother and daughter went to one rest room and the husband to the other. When Harry returned with Darya, he didn't see the husband or wife, but he saw the daughter being hurried to the car by two strangers.

He shouted "Attack!" as he and Darya rushed the two abductors. Darya made contact first by knocking one culprit down and hovering over him as Harry tackled the other one and dared him to get up.

In the meantime, the encounter had attracted attention, and the husband and wife were found in the restrooms unharmed—except perhaps by an overdose of chloroform. There happened to be an Alabama patrol car at the rest stop, so the kidnappers' careers were cut short. After a brief respite, the family continued their trip west. Needless to say, the number of passengers remained unchanged!

38

The legal suit against the college by the Keys family took a strange turn last week. When the Keys' attorney met with ours, our attorney showed theirs a copy of the letter that Harry Selby had written me. He informed their attorney that if the family insisted on pursuing their suit against the college, the college would be obligated to investigate the contents of the letter and to bring charges if applicable. The Keys' attorney said that he would consult with his clients and would be in touch.

The outcome was that the Keys' attorney met with the family, showed them the letter and agreed to meet with them again for their decision. They not only missed the appointment but apparently had left town. Our attorney checked and found that no Marsha Keys had been buried by a Watkinsville mortuary and there were no Keys working for the US Park Service. It may not have been a scam, but it is certainly a mystery!

At least, the old smoke tower has been spared. Instead of being a reminder of a tragedy, it should be remembered as the contribution of a vagabond and his dog to its preservation.

39

Dress rehearsal for *Night Must Fall* went very well, but I think it was opening night that broke the ice. Yancy had continued taking his leather hat box "home" with him. On opening night, he went around to all the dressing rooms distributing "break-a-leg" presents to the cast. Where did he carry them? In the leather hat box! At least the cast saw the inside of the forbidden prop. The show played well, and the smothering scene with blackout and strike was flawless. Diana had a show to be proud of. The remainder of the run was successful and the Thomebeh Society had members at every performance. I think that they were pleased with our added contribution to their generous gift.

The closing performance of *Night Must Fall* will be remembered for another reason: an astronomical anomaly that the entire area witnessed. It was first thought to be some sort of airship since it seemed to be traveling from the western horizon. However, as it crossed our lake, its shape was revealed to be a huge disk that glowed from within. There was no sound as the disk approached the smoke tower, hovered above it, and then resumed its trek east. No one thought about examining the smoke tower—they were more concerned about verifying what they had seen with others.

The following morning, one of the physical plant's men was checking the smoke tower's access door and found that it had been welded shut.

What was the apparition and what was its origin? What did it mean? For one thing, it sealed the smoke tower. For another, it seemed to suggest that the possibility existed that Ashley's putative extra-terrestrial "encounter" was true. And since the apparition was headed in the direction of the Thomebeh Mosque Headquarters, was it a rendez-vous or just a happenstance?

Anything is possible . . .

PART TWO

40

When it was discovered that the access door of the smoke tower had been welded shut after the "disk" hovered atop the tower, there was a feeling of gratitude on the Nunnery campus. Although they knew nothing about Ashley Bowman's adventure, they were aware of the court case against the college in which the Keys family claimed that if the smoke tower had been sealed, their daughter's death could have been prevented. Consequently, the campus suspected nothing when the "disk" was headed in the direction of the Thomebeh Society's headquarters.

I could not help but suspect that any "extraterrestrial" visitors had their own agenda, which involved sealing the tower. What could they have deposited in the tower that they wanted concealed? Perhaps if we knew more about the events leading up to the events . . .

First, why was Ashley Bowman selected to be abducted from all those in the freshman class? Was it something she had done, or did it involve her family? Was the Thomebeh Society involved in the selection? Had her mother or a relative attended Nunnery? Her parents said that night at the *Yerma* performance that they had just been out of town during the fall, and had just moved to Augusta. Perhaps they had moved because Ashley would be at Nunnery College?

Since most of the questions concerned one person, I had asked Ashley to come by my office.

She was prompt and anxious to learn why I wanted to speak to her. I assured her that it was nothing that she had done; I was just interested in the background of some events that took place in the fall.

"Since it is generally considered true that you were abducted last fall by extraterrestrial beings, do you have any idea why you were selected from the freshman class? Had you been involved in anything that could have made you a candidate?"

"Nothing," was her response. "Don't you think that I haven't asked myself that since it happened?"

"Did you see anyone while you were held hostage, except the creatures?"

"No," was her answer.

"No human beings?" I reiterated.

"None," she responded.

"Then, I'll ask about your family," I continued. "Have any members of your family ever attended Nunnery College?"

"Not to my knowledge," she replied.

"Had you ever heard of the Thomebeh Society before coming to Nunnery?" I continued.

"A few years ago, When the society was sponsoring a research committee to determine whether the Behemoth was real or mythical—like the unicorn. It was in my school newspaper. However, it never said why the society was interested."

I enlightened her by explaining that "Thomebeh" was an anagram of Behemoth, which is the society's mascot.

It seemed that the selection of Ashley by the ET was arbitrary unless the Thomebeh Society was involved to a degree that I had yet to discover.

Now, about the sealing of the smoke tower: the extraterrestrials may be tuned into the happenings on campus, and the campus has the right to be appreciative for the gesture that was attributed to them, but I am suspicious that our visitors had an ulterior motive. What could they have placed in the chimney? Of course, I am at a disadvantage since I know nothing of alien culture. What little we know we owe to Ashley, who was abducted and held by them. We know that they can appear and disappear at will, administer a drug that can conceal mode of transportation, and can speak English. After all, Ashley had been told, "Just do it!"

What if we unsealed the access door and found nothing? We would be back where we first were—with an unsealed tower!

41

Our third play would be presented next semester after Christmas. It would be directed by our "colleague of letters," in the auditorium of the Fine Arts Building. She had chosen *Phaedra,* by Jean Racine (1639–1699). It was no surprise that she had chosen a French play since her Ph.D. was in French Drama. If she could have, I'm certain that she would have presented the play in French!

Phaedra is based on the Greek play *Hippolytus* by Euripides, written in 428 B.C. Racine was also influenced by Seneca, a Spanish scholar who went to Rome as Nero's tutor and wrote his own versions (in Latin) of many Greek tragedies. His plays introduced ghosts, bloody deeds, gory descriptions and the 5-act structure that greatly influenced Shakespeare and other Elizabethan dramatists.

In the 5th Century B.C., that "golden century" of cultural achievement, Greek theatre was born, developed and matured. Each spring, in honor of Dionysus, the god of fertility (and wine), a playwriting contest was held. Since it was a religious festival, it is not surprising that Greek deities appear in many Greek tragedies. So it was with *Hippolytus.* The play is about the rivalry of two goddesses. The setting is the palace center stage with an altar on either side: one to Aphrodite, the goddess of love; one to Artemis, the virgin goddess of the hunt. Aphrodite is angry because Hippolytus, son of Theseus, King of Athens, will not pay homage to her. All Hippolytus cares about is hunting and remaining chaste like Artemis. Even worse, he possesses *hubris* (the trait of arrogant pride). Aphrodite plans his destruction by making Phaedra, his stepmother, fall madly in love with him. When Hippolytus learns of this, he is appalled for two reasons: he is against love (or sex) and Phaedra is his father's wife. When Phaedra is rejected, she fears that Hippolytus will tell the King, who has been away for ten years, but is returning. She goes into the palace and hangs herself, but leaves a letter accusing Hippolytus of attempting to seduce her.

The King flies into a rage and drives his son into exile; he also calls upon Neptune to destroy Hippolytus. Riding near the sea, a sea monster frightens his son's horses and he is dragged along the rocks. His dying body is brought back to his father and Artemis appears from a *deus ex machina.*

If you do not know too much about Greek drama, you probably know this term as a cheap literature solution. It literally means "god of the machine," and was a piece of stage machinery, like a crane, that could lower an actor onto the stage, symbolizing divine intervention. Artemis descends and explains that Hippolytus is an innocent victim of Aphrodite's jealousy and desire for vengeance, as Hippolytus dies.

It is easy to understand why Racine's *Phaedra* differed from the *Hippolytus* of Euripides. In the two thousand years since the Greek version, Christianity had replaced the gods of Mt. Olympus. One of the characteristics of the French mind during this neoclassic period was the passion for reducing life to a system of rules, regulations and logic. Tragedy in general could not portray contemporary events and there were many other restrictions. From a modern point of view, one wonders what freedom remained to French classic tragedy?

Actually a great deal. *The dramatist could, if he had the ability, portray human emotion.* While many playwrights of the period were inhibited by neoclassic restrictions, Jean Racine was not. In general, Racine possessed a natural sense of order and good taste that made the classic form, not a matter of restriction, but an expression of his natural style.

In *Hippolytus,* by Euripides, Phaedra may be considered a victim since Aphrodite made her fall in love with Hippolytus, her stepson. In *Phaedra,* there are no goddesses fighting over Hippolytus, and the lonely woman falls madly in love with her stepson because her husband the King has been gone for 10 years. When the King is reported dead, Phaedra decides to tell Hippolytus of her love. He is appalled by the confession and storms offstage. Shortly after, Phaedra learns that the news of the King's death was a mistake and fears that Hippolytus will tell the King her secret. When the King reaches the palace, she refuses his embrace and runs away. He questions the nurse who, to protect her mistress, tells the King that Hippolytus attempted to rape Phaedra. He flies into a rage and when his son is summoned, he denies the charge. (Then—off the record—Racine was probably envious of a certain Elizabethan playwright who was quoted all over Europe. When it occurred to Racine that there wasn't a single line in *Phaedra* that was quotable, he decided to give Hippolytus a few "bon mots" to accompany his denial: "There are some truths too true to tell.")

Unmoved, the King banishes him from the kingdom and invokes Neptune to destroy his son, as he did in *Hippolytus.* Fortunately, we don't see the carnage; we just hear the graphic description. Instead of a *deus ex machina,* Phaedra, having taken poison, views what is left of Hippolytus, admits that he was innocent, and then dies.

Since the set should suggest the facade of a palace, it would not be feasible to attempt that type of staging in an arena theatre, which explains why the proscenium stage of the auditorium had been selected. It consisted of a high facade of the palace on stage left with platforms, steps and columns which would permit Phaedra to "chew the scenery" when necessary. On stage right was a smaller set, a pavilion which Hippolytus frequents when he is with Aricie. With our strip lights and projections on the cyclorama, we would be able to provide impressive visual effects to complete the *mise-en-scène.*

42

The Thomebeh's tie-in with the extraterrestrials was circumstantial at best. It has been established that Ashley Bowman had probably been abducted and held for a week or so at an undisclosed location. Later it was learned from the Thomebeh's attorney that the Society was happy to have provided quarters for Ashley's acclimation to college life back in the fall. Since the attorney was acquainted with the arrangement, it seemed possible that she could have had prior knowledge of any liaison between the Society and the celestial visitors. With that in mind, I phoned Ms. Celia Hemphill for an appointment. She was most gracious and said that she would be on campus for a meeting with the President in the morning and would be glad to come by my office in the early afternoon. I thanked her and immediately began organizing an agenda.

The attorney arrived just before 2 P.M. After formalities, I attempted to explain how I became involved in the affair. I then described Ashley's version of what happened when she returned to her dorm room after the "Rat" ceremony—the blinding light, her fainting and awaking in a strange room with no doors, and including her experience with the "little creatures" who could appear and disappear at will.

The attorney listened intently and eventually asked, was Ashley bedridden in the strange room?

I admitted that I had no idea since she never shared that bit of information.

After a pause, Ms. Hemphill said that she wasn't aware of the Society's hospitality until she had been given the contents of the letter that she had delivered to me.

I then asked if she had any explanation concerning the so-called "little creatures?"

"None," she responded. "However, the Society does have a staff that is qualified to take care of various infirmities. The illusion of the 'little creatures,' " she continued, "could be attributed to the hallucinatory effects of certain drugs."

My response was that it seems like whoever, or whatever, instigated this abduction was clever enough to conceal the method of transportation by inducing fainting and/or administering a knockout drug.

The attorney conceded that I was right, apologized for not being of more help and departed.

Apparently Ms. Hemphill was an "outsider" as much as I was.

43

I was disappointed that I had learned about the Thomebeh's possible alliance with the celestial visitors. I had given Ms. Hemphill a chance to contribute some information when I inquired about the "little creatures." Her response consisted of a lecture on hallucination. What really needed was an interview with a staff member of the Thomebeth Society. How could that be worked out? If a question could not be arranged perhaps local residents might have observed "encounters." I put this inquiry on the back burner in favor of professional obligations.

Try as I might, the following week I found myself driving to the outskirts of Camon, and on the road to the Thomebeh's headquarters. I was surprised how isolated the mosque-like structure was. It seemed that there were no houses within a half mile of the Society's headquarters. These were farm houses and I stopped at the first one. Since it was winter, the inhabitants were indoors. I had concocted a spiel that should give credence to my inquiry. I asked if they had seen any sort of an aircraft in the vicinity of the Thomebeh headquarters recently?

"Not recently," was the reply. "But there was a lot of activity in the fall and also a couple of weeks ago. There wasn't any sound, but the animals were upset."

"Did you see anything?" I inquired.

"Nothing," my informant said. "But the sky was all lit up."

I thanked them and visited three other homes in the vicinity. I received virtually the same response from all of them. I had my answer—or did I? All of those people apparently experienced the same "encounter." Or they were all well-coached!

I got in my car and headed back to campus. As my investigation had accomplished little or nothing, I supposed I would just have to wait for an epiphany!

44

Since the Keys family had apparently forsaken Watkinsville and abandoned their suit against the college, there was little talk concerning the smoke tower except the mysterious sealing of the chimney one night. (Not everyone witnessed the disk or its hovering over the smoke tower—but even if they didn't see it, they believed it anyway.)

I don't know if there was any effort made to locate the elusive family. At the present time, there were no charges against them—except possibly their attorney's fee.

I don't know how diligent the Camon police are, but it is possible that they would check the Internet to see if the Keys family had perpetrated similar scams. (I just hope that they hadn't sacrificed other daughters!)

It is impossible to speculate on the activities of the Keys family without remembering the vigilance that the vagabond, Harry Selby, and his dog contributed to the exposure of their scheme. There hadn't been any account of the activities of the duo since their rescuing at the rest stop in Alabama. Apparently they continued to enjoy the hospitality of their hosts—as if they had a choice!

It wasn't exactly an epiphany, but part of the extraterrestrial mystery was solved by the physical plant's manager. He wasn't aware that the employee who discovered the sealing of the access door did not know that the manager had ordered the project done two days before. He apparently became suspicious when he overheard talk about a "hovering aircraft magically sealing the tower."

I doubt if many actually witnessed the event—but stories like this spread very quickly! For my epiphany to be completed, a logical explanation of the extra-terrestrial encounters would be appreciated.

45

Registration for the second semester was in January; the Admissions Office would send each departmental chairperson the names of students who had expressed interest in becoming majors in their departments. There were only three names on my memo, but one of the names was Marsha Keys! I immediately called Admissions to find out where the student was from? When I was told Watkinsville, GA, I had prayed that it would be elsewhere!

But it wasn't.

According to the Watkinsville telephone directory, there was only one family of Keys listed, and that was the family that had been suing the college before they left town.

I racked my brain, conjuring up every possible scenario to explain this anomaly. In the fall, I had come face to face with a student whom I *thought* to be dead; now I must meet a student that I *knew* to be dead: all of the vital statistics matched!

True, I never saw Marsha Keys dead, and as far as I knew, *I never saw her alive.* Obviously, this was some mistake. If this was the real Marsha Keys, then who was the person masquerading under that name who had wound up in the Camon city morgue? As I recalled, the autopsy determined that the corpse was a thirty-year-old female, but why did this Marsha Keys, a freshman, have to be from Watkinsville?

During the conclusion of the fall semester, I should have been busy with final exams and term papers, but I was distracted by the knowledge that I would be meeting with the namesake of the smoke tower victim. I doubted that the Admissions Office was even aware of the actual identity of the corpse after it was discovered that it wasn't Ashley Bowman. We all seemed to have one-track minds.

I had planned to go by the Campus Security Office before I received the memo from Admissions to find out if Jason Cabot had heard anything further about the Keys family from their attorney. I really had a good excuse this time!

I was in luck: Jason was in his office. I told him about the memo from Admissions alerting me about an entering student who as registering for the second semester, claiming to be interested in a theatre major. I could tell that Jason was wondering why I should be sharing this bit of trivia with him. I then told him that the student's name was Marsha Keys and she was from Watkinsville!

His demeanor changed as he asked me to repeat the memo.

I began, but he interrupted and said that he would call their attorney in case he had any information. He dialed, but there was no answer. He then told me that he would let me know what he had learned. (At least the ball was rolling.) I thanked him and departed.

46

During the Christmas holidays, the students go home, the faculty occasionally frequent their offices, the staff vacates the campus (for all practical purposes), and the physical plant and Security are reduced to skeleton crews. Since the campus is virtually deserted, it's the perfect time to take care of postponed chores without being disturbed. Anyway, that's the theory, but the interim is not always that predictable.

For instance, on the first morning, I received an E-mail from the publisher of the translation of *Phaedra* that had been selected by the director, telling us that this translation was no longer available to university institutions. There were other translations and adaptations, one in rhymed couplets and another so "correct" that it attempted the translation of the tragedy in alexandrine verse: a 12-syllable line.

Since the theatre staff had dispersed, it became my lot to attempt to rectify the problem. We had a copy of the script, so we could Xerox copies for the cast. However, not only was that illegal, but in order to stage it, we would be required to pay a royalty for a play that we lacked permission to present!

I went through my collection of scripts to see if I had a translation that I had overlooked. I found four scripts of *Phaedra* that I pulled to compare with the withdrawn version. Of course these were older scripts that might not still be in print, but might possibly be available to duplicate.

One of the *Phaedra* scripts in my collection was very similar to the withdrawn translation. (In fact, I thought parts of it were actually better.) Anyway, I got a letter off to the publisher, but I'll not be holding my breath in getting a response: his address didn't even have a zip code!

I dropped both of my theatre colleagues a note advising them that the publisher had withdrawn the *Phaedra* translation that we had decided on, but that I had found an obscure version which might be a possibility. I enclosed my copy of that script with my note to the director, our "Colleague of Letters." I then attempted to tackle the chores that had been neglected.

It was fortunate that the chores didn't require a great deal of thought because my mind wandered to the meeting I would have with "Marsha Keys" after Christmas. A student enrolling at Nunnery College, named Marsha Keys, had to be a coincidence; but to be coming from Watkinsville, GA, was mind-boggling, to say the least. There had to be a rational explanation, but without any clues, I was at a loss.

47

Speaking of surprises, I received another one at the campus Post Office during the holidays. The publisher that I was afraid had gone out of business answered my letter with some good news: the script was still in print and the required royalty was less than our original choice! I was so certain that our director would like it, that I immediately ordered twelve scripts for the cast and crew, with the request for permission to present *Phaedra* in January.

I assumed that Jason Cabot wouldn't be around during the holidays, but I received a memo from him sharing what he had learned about the Keys family from their attorney. He and the police had gotten a search warrant to enter the Keys' former house and discovered that the family apparently had other names that they used, or were continuing to use. Those names were added to the "wanted" lists. The two investigators found evidence that the Keys family had previously been in the funeral business. Since there was no record of a burial of a Marsha Keys in Watkinsville by either of the funeral homes, and with the family formerly in the business, the possibility was that when the family left, they carried an embalmed body with them!

Wow!

With the condition that the body was in, one of the family had better be good at reconstruction!

48

The second semester was at hand. (I refuse to call it the Spring Semester since winter was still with us.) I had rehearsed this interview a dozen times during the Christmas vacation, but this was for real. I was in my office to welcome Marsha Keys from Watkinsville, GA. Fortunately few if any of the students had even heard of a Marsha Keys—just some of the key administrators. (No pun intended.)

When the prescribed time approached, I wondered if she would keep the appointment. My apprehension subsided when there was a knock on my office door at the exact time listed on the memo. I answered the door and invited her to have a seat as I returned to my desk chair. I introduced myself and asked if she'd had a nice fall?

"Except for moving," she replied. "It took us all fall to move and get settled in our new home."

I admit that I was impressed by this Marsha's demeanor and appearance. True, I never saw the other Marsha—dead or alive—but this one would be a rival, and she was certainly not 30 years of age.

Although I knew that other members of the Keys family had other names, I thought that I would introduce the subject by telling her that there was another Keys family in Watkinsville until recently and that they also had a daughter named Marsha.

"Really?" was her only response.

I didn't go into details. Since it didn't involve her, there was no reason to burden her with the baggage.

"By the way, are you a transfer or a freshman? The Admissions Office didn't specify."

"I'll be a freshman," she replied. "Our moving prevented my matriculating in the fall."

Impressive, I thought: *her parents must be in education*. I continued by asking about her previous experience in theatre?

She said that she liked both acting and the technical aspects of theatre. She especially liked set design, but her acting experience included both contemporary and classical roles.

I commented on the variety of plays that her high school provided.

She corrected me by saying it hadn't been in high school where she got her experience, but the local community theatre.

"And where was this?" I inquired.

"Sarasota, Florida," she answered.

As I was preparing to ask why she chose Nunnery, she volunteered the answer: she had heard that the head of the Theatre Department at Nunnery College was an expert at pyrotechnics, which she wanted to learn more about.

I told her that I had been the Technical Director of *Unto These Hills*, an outdoor production at Cherokee, NC, for a number of years and had learned to use dynamite, black powder, and squibs to make flash pots, explosions, etc. Fortunately, I'd been able to utilize some of this know-how in our stage plays. Although I don't teach pyrotechnics per se, I would be happy to share what I had learned.

I told her about *Phaedra*, the play that we would be holding auditions for next, and welcomed her as a major.

After she had departed, I began to wonder what I had agreed to. Was she interested in pyrotechnics for the stage, or a more sinister agenda?

49

The new scripts for *Phaedra* arrived by the time the staff had returned. I noticed that the audition notices were posted, so apparently our "Colleague of Letters" was reconciled to our using the new script. I plan to tell her to be on the lookout for our new theatre major. I hesitated revealing her name, but chances are that she would be oblivious to extraneous matters.

I reported to Jason at Security my interview with the "new" Marsha Keys, that she and her family had just moved to Watkinsville from Sarasota, FL and that I had already told her that there had been *another* Marsha Keys in Watkinsville, but didn't go into detail. He thanked me and said I had handled it well. (I don't know why, but I thought it prudent not to share *why* she had selected Nunnery College.)

Our proscenium is 40′ wide, but we usually mask it in to 38′ and trim the height at 16′. Since I wanted the facade of the palace to be 24′ high (out of sight to the audience) I would either have to batten together two 12′ flats, or 16′ and 8′ flats. I chose the latter since 12′ flats are more in demand. In front of the facade would be a landing the width of the facade and 3′ deep. Five steps, 12" deep by 6" high would provide the escape from the landing. Most of the construction had been done previously (we save everything) so it was just a matter of fitting them all together. Of course, there would be the task of painting a structure this size, but it had to be constructed first.

There was a good turn-out for the *Phaedra* auditions. The director had found two men for the King and Hippolytus. The role of the tutor, Thévamènes could be changed to a woman.

I know that Marsha Keys attended the auditions. I thought she might play Aricie, the love interest of Hippolytus, but I wasn't casting the play.

I hadn't seen Ashley Bowman yet. I don't even know if she auditioned. She could play Phaedra, but the director, while she likes to spread the choice roles around if possible, won't cast an incompetent. We have no compunction about a racial mix, if it doesn't distract from the theme of the play. For instance, when I was at the University of IL. a few years ago, the Theatre Dept. often supplied technical assistance to the Music Dept. when it presented an opera in our theatre. One year, the Music Dept. wanted to present a new opera version of Shakespeare's *Romeo and Juliet.* In casting the opera, the best performer who could sing Romeo was an African American. Since the entire cast was Caucasian, when Capulet objected to his daughter having an affair with a Montague, the fact that this Romeo was an African American confused the reason that he was a member of a rival family.

50

Now that the matter of two Keys families in Watkinsville was cleared up—at least one family had left town, presumably taking their embalmed daughter with them; the other with no connection moving from Florida, and enrolling their daughter Marsha in Nunnery College.

I determined to pursue my investigation of any liaison between the Thomebeh Society and the extraterrestrial phenomenon. Instead of approaching the query indirectly via their attorney and neighbors, I decided to make an appointment with the Society itself. I assumed that they would have an administrative assistant to answer the phones and schedule appointments. I phoned the Society several times before it was answered by a male. I identified myself and requested an appointment with a representative of the Society. He was extremely courteous but said that it would be difficult to assemble the entire Society. What was the nature of the interview?

I explained that it had to do with the Society hosting the acclimation of Ashley Bowman last fall. I added that it did not have to be the entire Society.

The gentleman asked for my phone number and said that he would notify me if he could arrange a meeting.

I thanked him and hung up, certain that he would be calling the college to check my credentials before attempting to schedule an appointment. I returned to campus and alerted my student assistant to take the message if the Society called, or better still, page me out of class if the call came in a morning.

I returned to my daily routine fully expecting no response to my request. If I were right, what should be my next maneuver?

I went backstage to prepare some work for the tech crew when they would arrive later in the afternoon. I had just unlocked the shop door when the student assistant came to inform me that I had a phone call from a man at the Thomebeh Society. The caller wasn't still holding but left a message that he had made my appointment for 10:00 the next morning. I thanked the news bearer and attempted to organize the lab, but my mind was distracted by the faux pas that I had requested.

After a night of tossing and turning, I had breakfast in the Snack Bar and sought some solitude in my office before leaving for the Thomebeh Society headquarters. I still lacked a rational approach. If I questioned them about having a liaison with any extraterrestrial visitors, and they were innocent, I would surely be thought deranged; but I was at a loss as to how to approach the subject subtly without exposing my own misconceptions. I finally decided to "play it by ear."

I turned into the headquarters and drove around to the rear parking lot, where I counted over a dozen cars there, so perhaps I would meet with the full Society?

I walked around to the front door and was surprised that I was greeted by Celia Hemphill, the Society's attorney. She took me to the main room with the chandelier and the large round table. All 12 Thomebeh members were already seated and the attorney waved me to the nearest empty chair while she crossed to the far side. She then welcomed me and explained to the group who I was, even though I had been a guest there previously. (It had been at least three years since I was here and there could easily have been a partial turnover.)

"Professor McAmby approached me before Christmas concerning this matter, but I was unable to be of help," Ms. Hemphill began. (Obviously, the administrative assistant had alerted her to the subject of the appointment.) "I shall now turn the meeting over to our guest," she added and took her seat.

I thanked her and the Society for granting this audience. Not wishing to broach the subject without some preamble, I thanked the Society for providing accommodations for Ashley Bowman this past fall. In fact, I told them, this meeting has to do with Ashley's impression of that week. It began with her abduction—Ashley's term, not mine.

She was in her dorm room when it suddenly became so bright that she apparently fainted. When she came to, she was in a strange room "without doors." She was visited by "strange little creatures" who could appear and disappear at will. I admitted that the fainting and the relocation could have affected her perception, but before she was returned to her dorm, she was given an injection that "blocked out" any remembrance of that procedure. I had considered this entire experience to be a hallucination brought on by stress and fatigue (since Ashley swore that no drugs were involved), until last November on the closing night of *Night Must Fall,* when a number of us witnessed a celestial aberration—a disk-shaped flying object that came from the east, crossed our lake, and hovered over our smoke tower before moving in the direction of this building.

"I have questioned your neighbors," I said. "They remembered seeing a bright light that night, but couldn't pinpoint it. The question is, does the Thomebeh Society have any alliance with an extra-terrestrial entity?"

I started to mention that it was thought that when the "disk" hovered over the smoke tower, it had sealed the access door, but it was later learned that the physical plant had already done that two days earlier. It then occurred to me that *the disk didn't know that!* Perhaps it dropped something in the tower for dispersing, but now it was sealed in! Before I could decide whether or not to share my dilemma, one of the Thomebeh sisters began the response to my question.

"Professor McAmby, I remember you from the last time you visited the Society. I believe that you and your colleague were asking our Society if we were the same society that was chartered in 1850, when Nunnery College was the Camon female Liberal Arts College for Women."

I started to reply, but realized that it wasn't a question.

She continued by repeating that the Society was happy to have been able to provide accommodations for Ashley Bowman during her acclimation to college life. The sisters then returned to my question with the admission that the Thomebeh Society had indeed had dealings with "other worlds" several times since their inception.

"In what way?" I inquired.

"Our archives weren't specific," she replied. "The only encounter that we are familiar with is the current one," she added.

"Are you allowed to discuss it?" I asked.

The group members looked around at each other. Another member spoke. "I suppose so: we weren't told *not* to—"

"Just how did it happen, then?" I inquired.

Another member joined in "We were seated around this table waiting for our dinner when the room suddenly became very bright, somewhat as Miss Bowman described, except no one fainted. We were told that this room would be needed and that we should go to other quarters. We were not to enter this room because an Ashley Bowman from Nunnery College would occupy it. Food should be provided and placed outside the door."

"Did you see who had instructed you?" I asked.

"Like I said, there was such a bright light, we could see nothing. When the room returned to normal, there was no one here," she answered.

"And you saw no one, but you left food outside the door for a week?"

"That's right. A week or so later, we noticed that the food was untouched and no one was in the room," another member volunteered.

I had one other question: "Did you ever see or hear any sort of unusual flying object while the room was occupied, or later in the fall?"

"Not while the room was occupied, but in November, probably that's what you were referring to, we were visited by a disk-shaped object."

"What was its purpose?" I asked, attempting to conceal my enthusiasm.

"We never learned why, but Ashley Bowman was not a random selection. Anyway, the return visit that night was to leave a token of appreciation. Of course, this is not to leave this room."

I started to ask, "What in the world was it then?" When the absurdity of the question dawned on me. "What was it?" I finally asked.

The question was answered by twelve voices in unison, "The Fountain of Youth!"

I thanked my hosts and departed, but my drive back to

campus was a confused one: why hadn't I asked to see that "token of appreciation?" Was it really a fountain, or was it bottles of an elixir to drink or bathe in; or better still, a concentrate that you would add to bath water?

What would they do with it: just use it, or perhaps have it analyzed and attempt to manufature it themselves? At this edge in time, this formula would be more valuable than the medieval alchemist's secret of turning base metals into gold!

51

I almost wished that I hadn't pursued the Thomebehs' alliance with the extraterrestrials. All I was seeking was their possible association, not knowledge of a gift that could be cataclysmic. My only solace was that my personal knowledge of the gift would have no effect on its use.

Some solace: Waiting for the other shoe to drop! And I couldn't even share this with anyone, so on to the brink!

One thing I would do is contact Ashley Bowman. Since the Society made a point that her abduction was not a random selection, perhaps she could recall some incident that could be the key as to why she had been involved with extraterrestrials.

I had my theatre assistant contact Ashley and ask her to come by my office. (I had no idea how she would do it: by phone, e-mail or carrier pigeon.)

A few minutes later, my assistant informed me that Ashley would come by my office right after lunch.

I made a point of being in my office before meeting my tech crew.

Ashley was as good as her word: she knocked on my door at 1:15. I asked her to come in (my office isn't large enough to require shouting).

I told her that I had met with the Thomebeh Society concerning her stay at their headquarters this past fall.

"Was something wrong?" Ashley asked. "I admit that I wasn't very coherent while I was there. In fact, I didn't even know where I was."

I told her that it didn't have anything to do with her

stay—"but the society is of the opinion that your abduction wasn't just a random selection."

"What does that mean?" she asked.

I told her that the extraterrestrials must have had a reason to select her. I asked her was there anything in her past that seemed strange or "other worldly"?

"No, nothing like that," she replied.

I assured her that it didn't have to be that severe: Just a feeling, a flash—*anything* out of the ordinary.

"What about dreams? I've had some weird ones," she confessed.

I asked if they were recurrent?

"Not really," she said, "just weird."

I was ready to give up. This young lady was so normal that it must have been a random selection. I then thought of one avenue that I hadn't tried. I gave her my assurance that this was between her and me: had she ever used marijuana, peyote, or any hallucinogenic or recreational drugs?

"Never," was her answer.

I thanked her for coming by and for answering my questions, both general and personal. Also, I asked her to let me know if she remembered anything that might suggest why the "aliens" had selected her.

52

I dropped by the director's office to learn how the "new" Marsha Keys had done at auditions. She reported "very well," in fact, Marsha had been cast in the Aricia role. (I didn't mention that that was my thinking—without knowing who had auditioned.)

"Who is playing Phaedra?" I asked.

"Sandra Billings, a senior. Ashley Bowman didn't audition, and in a way, I'm glad. She would have been a great Phaedra, but two leads in one year for a freshman is a bit much," she confessed.

I told her that I agreed, and departed. I then began to wonder why Ashley hadn't auditioned. Although appearing in a school production wasn't mandatory even for drama majors, it was a wise practice. It even occurred to me that Ashley Bowman had yet to declare her major.

I could have covered all of these things at our meeting if I hadn't been so preoccupied with the reason for her "abduction."

Since I was visiting this afternoon, I decided to go by our infamous smoke tower to inspect the welding of the access door by the maintenance crew. I had always assumed that the furnace conduits were once attached to the smoke tower at the base of the chimney. To my surprise, they were attached a good ten feet above the base—and still were!

That meant that if the hovering disk had placed "something" in the smoke tower to disburse via the access door (not knowing that it had been sealed) it could now travel through the conduits to the dormant furnaces, and then possibly on through the buried steam pipes all over campus. Something else to worry about. (Ignorance really is bliss!)

On the way back to my office, I passed part of our "golden pond" and glanced over at the floating island of alligator weeds. I happened to notice a piece of clothing resting on the weeds. Katharine Floyd of the Biology Department told me years ago that in order for a corpse to be discovered there, it would be necessary for it to be supported among the weeds like Moses in the bulrushes. Nevertheless, I unhitched a boat (or whatever the term is), and rowed out to the floating island as I had done when Ashley Bowman was missing in the fall. (I had apparently already forgotten my adoption of the "ignorance is bliss" slogan.)

As I approached the floating island, I could see the garment draped over a cluster of alligator weeds close to its edge. The question was not how it got there, but *why?* It had been placed there either to attract attention, or possibly related to a more sinister action. At any rate, I decided to remove it to avoid it from attracting more attention. There was a cane fishing pole in the bottom of the boat that aided me in its recovery. That was when I discovered blood on the garment! Before weighing the pros and cons of my action, I placed the garment in the boat and rowed toward the pier.

When I docked the boat, I removed my jacket to cover the folded garment. It was a long-sleeved blouse on which the figured fabric obscured the dried blood on both a sleeve and the front of the blouse.

I put my cache in a storage box in the costume closet, as I saw no reason to involve Security unless some mayhem was reported. Since the blouse had been so blatantly displayed, it was probably a prank anyway. I only hoped that the Bard's "Much Ado About Nothing" determination was as valid that day as it was in the 17th century!

53

I sat in on one of the rehearsals for *Phaedra* and was pleasantly surprised that our director wasn't demanding that the actors adhere to the alexandrine verse: a 12-syllable line. (She could have, since her Ph.D. was in French literature. She also could have coaxed the cast to perform *Phaedra* in the French neo-classical manner, and bored the audience. . . .) The modern audience is more interested in the story and characters than in the style that the play was presented 800 years ago.

Sandra Billings, the senior playing Phaedra, was well cast. It inspired me to really give her a great set to emote on. The Aricia scenes weren't scheduled, so I couldn't observe how Marsha Keys was coming along. The rest of the supporting cast was impressive. My tech crew and I had our work cut out for us.

The next afternoon, I was on stage with my crew when I heard a bark at the back of the auditorium. Just like the semester when we were building *Yerma*, Harry Selby was coming down the aisle.

"Look, the celebrities are coming home!" I shouted as I left the stage to meet them. The crew followed and greeted the dog.

As I shook Harry's hand, I added, "Your escapade made the news service."

"It was nothing," he replied, graciously. "I just went along for the excitement."

"Not according to the papers," I responded. "Where did you and Darya wind up?"

"Believe it or not, the family we were with were from

Clovis, New Mexico so I was able to go back and see the doctor's wife who'd given me Darya. She wasn't in very good health, but I was glad that I was able to say thank you again."

"How did you wind up back in Georgia?" I inquired.

"The same way I wind up anywhere," Harry replied. "I just stand by the side of the road with Darya, and go wherever my ride takes me."

I changed the subject by apologizing for not having more of the *Phaedra* set working. I pointed to where the palace facade would be, Aricia's pavilion.

"I once saw *Phèdre* (the French spelling) on a bare stage," he responded.

Becoming a bit peeved, I reacted with, "And I suppose the actors spoke in alexandrine verse!"

Harry's comeback was, "I didn't say it was good!"

The crew joined me in laughing at myself.

I then brought Harry up-to-date about the Keys family's exit when a copy of his letter was shown to their attorney. I even touched on the absence of a Marsha Keys burial in Watkinsville and the possibility that the family had left town carrying an embalmed but not buried member in their car. (I saw no reason to say that another Marsha Keys was enrolled at Nunnery this semester.)

As he and Darya were leaving, I thanked him again for his contribution in solving the smoke tower mystery plus possibly averting the college from being sued. (I would wager that Harry Selby's travels are more like a mission than an odyssey.)

54

It had been several weeks since the alien disk hovered over the smoke tower and there had been no adverse effects reported. Apparently my concern was needless. I recall that one of the observers that night facetiously suggested that it was probably being used as a rest room!

So far, there had been no report of any student being attacked, or treated at the infirmary. At any rate, I decided to take the blouse to Security—just to see if the "blood" was real. Unfolding the blouse in Jason Cabot's office, I described my seeing the garment draped over the alligator weeds on the floating island, after which I rowed out, recovered it, and placed it in our costume department. The office's testing kit determined that it was human blood, but didn't know exactly what to do next. Jason had me show him the exact spot where I found the blouse, so we rowed out to the alligator weeds, where he poked around for a while. Since there had been no report of a mishap, I supposed that he was looking for a body . . .

As we returned to the pier, he said that he would make certain no one from the college community was missing.

I assumed that forensic people could determine the DNA from the dried blood on the blouse; but they *couldn't match it* unless someone was missing. Pardon the cliché—but it takes two to tango.

My other pending concern was the Thomebeh Society's extraterrestrial gift. "The Fountain of Youth" has been sought in some form throughout the ages, more recently by Ponce de Leon in Florida. Since the "Fountain" has more or less been considered a myth, the search continues via cosmetics, injections and surgery. And as the "gift" is protected by secrecy, no one is sure if it's a tonic, a lotion, a bath—or none of the above.

It seems that the Thomebeh Society has two choices: share the gift or keep it for themselves. If they choose the first, it would mean having it analyzed and attempting to duplicate it—for profit. Since there had been no sudden advertising blitz for the Fountain of Youth, or any other similar name, chances are that the society was keeping it in the family.

Although I had only known about it since Christmas, the Society had received it in November. It is also possible or probable that the gift is amenable only to an alien culture. In that case, no news is definitely good news!

I was in my office after lunch when there was a knock on my door. When I said "Come in," Ashley Bowman entered.

"You said if I thought of something that might explain why I was selected for the abduction, to let you know," she said, getting immediately to the point.

"When I was in high school, I was watching *X-Files* with my father one Sunday night, and this episode was when Mulder's sister was visited by extraterrestrials and abducted. I told my father that the same thing had happened to me," Ashley continued. "He said I had never mentioned it before: It must have been a dream."

"Was it?" I asked.

"I don't think so," she replied, as she pulled down her collar. "See this little disque on the back of my neck? It wasn't there before that night."

"So you think that little figure marked you to be selected for the abduction last fall?" I asked.

"I don't see any other reason."

"But what was accomplished? What was their motive?" I questioned.

"The only thing I can think of, I was told to audition for *Yerma*," she replied.

"Well, we all benefited from that," I volunteered. "Incidentally—how did you communicate?"

"I just spoke," she said, "but the strange thing was that even though the little creatures didn't speak, I knew what they were thinking. I think it was telepathy or something."

Telepathy or something was probably right!

55

On Monday, the director of *Phaedra* informed me that Marsha Keys, who was playing Aricia, had missed several rehearsals. That was just before Jason Cabot called to tell me that he had discovered the missing student: a freshman named Marsha Keys. He then asked me why that name was familiar? I reminded him that I had told him that there was *another* Marsha Keys from Watkinsville. "Anyway," Jason said, "she has been missing for four days!"

As I was returning from the Post Office later, I noticed that he had his crew probing the entire floating island.

Apparently, after identifying the missing student, he collected enough DNA samples from her dorm room to match them with the blood DNA on the blouse. So now, we knew the identity of the victim—but not her whereabouts or physical condition.

My first thought was Harry Selby and possibly Darya, but I had no idea where he was or how to contact him. Besides, I didn't know if Afghans could even track. (If I ever see him again, I also want to ask him about flying disks and extraterrestrials. If anyone should know, he should. He has probably hitched a ride!)

The first week or so of the second semester, and we have a freshman missing. At least we won't have to look in the base of the smoke tower, since the access door has been sealed. The floating island of alligator weeds had been thoroughly searched. Of course, there was the lake itself with its untold accumulation which hasn't been drained in years. I'm certain that all the nooks and crannies from the fall search had been revisited. The only theory remaining was the obvious possibility that she was off campus—by choice or coercion.

I know it would be a delicate question to ask a student's family if she were at home—if she *weren't*. Of course if she were at home further search would be avoided. Unfortunately, questioning her friends, like the fall disappearance, would be fruitless because of the short time new arrivals were on campus. My only contribution would be to contact the Thomebeh Society in case they were providing accommodations for yet another student's "acclimation to college life." And if it were at the request of "alien neighbors," what gift of appreciation would the Society receive?

That afternoon, I really experienced *déjà vu:* the play's director asked me if she should ask Ashley Bowman to step in and play Aricia?

I pointed out that Ashley didn't even attend auditions.

She said she realized that, but the other cast members had suggested it.

"Why not ask her if she would understudy the role," I advised. "If Marsha does not return in time, then we'll let Ashley play it."

Our "Colleague of Letters" thanked me and said she would take care of it. After she left, I wondered how close Ashley and Marsha were? I'd never seen them together, which didn't necessary mean anything. Since they were both freshmen they had to be in the same dorm. And that didn't necessarily mean anything, either.

Before I could contact the Society, I received a call from Jason Cabot at Security. He said that Marsha's parents had been questioned and he learned that Marsha had been there earlier in the week, but had returned to campus. I asked if she had a car, he said she did—that the ruling about no cars for freshmen applied only during the fall semester. I mentioned the blood-stained blouse. His opinion was that it must have happened after she drove home.

I went ahead and phoned the Thomebeh Society. The administrative assistant insisted that no student was incarcerated there.

It still bothered me that the blood-stained blouse had been so blatantly displayed. It seemed to be either a challenge or a cry for help.

In my capacity, I seemed to have contributed my limit, so I returned to the construction of Phaedra's palace.

56

I had just unlocked the shop—I wanted to get organized before the tech crew arrived—when I heard the auditorium
door from the lobby opening. The visitors were none other
than Harry Selby and Darya!

"I hear you need some help," was his greeting.

"I don't know how you would know: I told no one," I
admitted.

"Telepathy, maybe—I've been known to possess it,"
was his response. "How can I be of help?"

"Come on down and I'll fill you in," was my invitation.

I shared all of the details of Marsha Keys' disappearance—including my discovery of the blood-stained blouse.

"Why does that name seem familiar?" he asked.

I explained that a freshman had entered the Nunnery
this semester bearing the same name as the body in the
smoke tower; she also came from Watkinsville, GA, but was
no relation.

He asked where the blouse was.

I told him, "In the Security office" and inquired,
"Why?"

"I just want Darya to smell it," he replied. "She had
rather chase someone down, but she has been successful at
tracking."

I took Harry and Darya over to Security and introduced them to Jason as the letter writer in the Keys case,
and explained his professional position. The blouse was
examined with Darya getting a "nose full." Jason asked if
Harry needed to take the blouse. Harry declined, saying
that Darya had a good sense memory.

I thanked Jason and arranged for the duo to have full

range of the campus, with lodging. I told Harry to come by any time; in fact, I had a matter to discuss with him.

I saw Harry and Darya head for the lake as I was returning to the theater.

I went by the *Phaedra* rehearsal that night, primarily to see if the director had contacted Ashley Bowman. The Aricia scene with Hippolytus was being rehearsed, with the "understudy." I was amazed how quickly she had learned the blocking and the lines—like she had been cast in the role. Why was that bothering me?

I hadn't heard anything from Jason or Harry Selby in a couple of days, but I saw no reason to bother Jason. If he had any news he would have called me. So I went ahead minding my own business—and wondering.

Apparently the college hadn't broadcast the news that a student was missing. I'm certain that the *Phaedra* cast didn't realize it. They probably thought that Marsha was sick and the understudy had been brought in—after all, they had suggested it. Security was investigating the incident, so there was no reason to advertise it. I had overlooked the spectacle of Harry and Darya roaming the campus, but I'll leave that explanation to Security.

So much had been going on lately, I had put aside Ashley Bowman's recollection of the outer space experience that the *X-Files* had evoked. I don't know if she had shown her father the slight disfigurement she supposedly had received in the space craft—it would be difficult to conceal without a collar. If one believed that Ashley was selected and abducted by extraterrestrials, one should accept that she was awarded a brand.

Notice to the Reader:

Chapter 54 contains my dissertation on the Fountain of Youth and the search for it through the ages. I was concerned about the Society's use of it, but more than that, I questioned whether their alien gift was even compatible for use on this planet. Since then, I realized that it was presumptive for me, a mere *Homo sapiens*, to attempt to evaluate beings that have mastered celestial navigation, refined telepathy, and used our restrooms (latrine humor also from Chapter 54). They could have researched our physiology and developed a Fountain of Youth that was applicable to our species.

57

I went by Security to find out if any progress had been made. Jason said the blood-stained blouse was useless except for supplying DNA. Darya had picked up the scent and followed it to the costume room and then to my office. I said of course, I had wrapped it in my jacket and taken it to the costume storage room, and then I took my jacket to my office. (Darya had tracked the blouse and then the jacket but not the victim.) I then asked if tracking was out then what clues is Harry following now?

"Intuition, I think," he replied. "That's about all we have."

"Have you located Marsha's car on campus?" I asked.

"No, which seems to suggest that she probably did not reach campus," he replied.

"But you said that since her parents never noticed her wound, it must have happened after she returned," I pointed out.

"You are right," he granted, "and it might be of some help if we knew why she went home that night."

I agreed, leaving that chore in his hands, and departed.

Why Marsha's car was gone if she had been attacked suggested two possibilities; she either went for medical attention, or her car was stolen and she remained on campus in an unknown condition. If the latter proved correct, Harry and Darya would surely find her.

A day later, Jason Cabot phoned me that since Marsha had not registered her car, he called her parents for the make and license number. While he had them on the line, he apologized and asked if they could tell him why she visited them that night? He then told them that her car had been abandoned in Valdosta, GA, but no blood was found in the car. Her parents said that she had come home to pick up some heavier clothes. He asked them if they could describe what she was wearing that night, and they described the blouse minus the blood!

"Well," I said, "that means that the victim is still on campus—dead or alive."

"Right," he responded. "Keep the faith."

Straight down US 75. He (or she) was probably headed for Florida. I wondered why it was abandoned. Apparently it wasn't wrecked, but why was I concerned about the car when my concern should be about Marsha Keys here on the campus of Nunnery College? I was forgetting that the campus was a part of the Nunnery estate of 240 acres, the majority of which was wooded with trails for both horses and pedestrians. I was confident that Harry and Darya were exploring the backwoods.

I still wondered why the blouse was so blatantly displayed on the floating island? There was no reason to advertise the assault. The perpetrator must have been an exhibitionist as well as an assailant and car thief.

When Jason told me that the abandoned car was discovered in Valdosta, I thought that it was headed for Florida. I had forgotten that Marsha had said that they had moved from Sarasota. It seemed there was a likelihood that the culprit was also from Sarasota, and that Marsha knew him. I made a point to call Security and to share my thinking with Jason and let him take it from there. I also suggested they find out if they knew any of the boys that she had dated in Florida? Jason thought it was a good idea and thanked me for the suggestion. At last we had a lead!

58

I was awaiting word about Jason's call to Marsha's parents about boyfriends of their daughter in Florida. If they could recall any names, Jason could have the Sarasota police do some investigating. Also, he might have something to report from Harry and Darya. I finally called; but he was out.

I started thinking about the blouse draped over the alligator weeds in the floating island. Suddenly it dawned on me that perhaps it wasn't the attacker but the victim who had hung it there to let her ordeal be known. The hoodlum had probably gone for the car while she was doing this. The question now was: where did she then go for refuge? Chances are, she would still be there, one way or another. (We still didn't know the severity of the wound.)

As I was preparing for my tech crew's lab, I was visited by Harry Selby and friend. I hadn't seen them since Security had taken charge. "Have you made any headway?" I queried.

"Well, we now know where she *isn't,*" he replied.

I then told him that I was beginning to think that the victim had displayed the blood-stained blouse to inform the campus that she had been attacked, and then sought shelter.

Harry admitted that my theory had merit and said that he would take the blouse to the lake and let Darya perceive the odor from non-bloody areas and see where that would lead her.

I wished the two good luck and returned to my work.

Jason Cabot called from Security later that afternoon.

He had heard from the Keys in Watkinsville. All the boys Marsha had dated came from good families and the Keys knew their parents. There had been one man that Marsha thought was stalking her. He wasn't a student and she knew him only as "Dave."

I told Jason that Harry and Darya had embarked on a new lead that looked promising. I then asked him if the information that the parents had provided would be of any help? He said probably not, unless "Dave" had a record and was recognizable by his first name only.

I tried putting myself in Marsha's place and wondered where I would go? There must have been a reason that she didn't go to the infirmary, where she could have been treated or sent to the hospital. She could have returned to her dorm room or suite. That would have been better than any other refuge she might have selected. What "wounds" did she wish to conceal? If she had removed her blouse, would she have been half-naked? She had gone to her home for more clothes—but had she worn any of them, or were they still in her car?

I heard about Harry and Darya's quest via the Security Office. They had located Marsha in the feed room at the equestrian stables. After providing Darya with an unbloodied section of the blouse, she led Harry to the stables and to the feed room. He called Security from the stables, and they sent transportation and help to move her to the infirmary.

I asked what condition was she in?

"Hungry and weak," he reported. The infirmary was puzzled about her wound. There was what looked like a bite on the left side of her neck. It had bled on her blouse and the right sleeve's blood was the result of her attempting to stop the flow by blotting it.

"Is she still at the infirmary?" I asked.

"No," he replied. "She was taken to the hospital. I'm trying to get in touch with the police in Sarasota to learn if they had been able to identify this Dave, the infirmary and the hospital need to know of any HIV, etc., that might require special treatment."

Such as "vampirism," I thought—*if that is a word!* The wound area certainly resembles the traditional type of attack. Of course, there is no data supporting the legend of the victim becoming a vampire—but who wants to be a smorgasbord?

Harry and Darya came by to say good-bye. I asked where were they headed?

"Wherever," was Harry's reply. "I'll have you know that I was offered a job with Security—with accommodations."

"You should have taken it," I advised.

"Perhaps, but it would tie me down," Harry replied. "If you ever need any help, let me know: I'm on your wave-length."

Believe it or not, I felt safer.

The Sarasota Police recognized Dave's name in their misdemeanor file, gave him a last name ("Adams") and compared his fingerprints with those in the stolen car in Valdosta: a perfect match. They now knew who the fugitive was and what he had done—but not his whereabouts!

Marsha Keys' family came down from Watkinsville when she was in the hospital. The details of the attack were still lacking, but her prognosis was good although she would have to undergo some reconstructive surgery. The police had yet to find and arrest Dave Adams, although they had come to Camon and with the Camon police had interviewed Marsha and inspected the crime scene.

I had attempted to re-create the scenario of Marsha's attack. Instead, I came up with a bevy of questions. When she pulled into the parking lot from her home, was "he" waiting for her there? How did "he" know she had gone to Watkinsville and would be returning that night? When she saw him, why did she even leave the car, and apparently accompany him out of the parking lot toward the lake? If he had been stalking her as she had told her parents, this would be their first time together. How was he able to overpower her and bite her neck? Had he come to find her in order to take her car? Nothing but questions! It would seem that he had her under a spell, and she came out of it only after he left.

59

It seemed that Marsha Keys would be recuperating for some time, so Ashley Bowman would be playing the role of Aricia in *Phaedra*. The rehearsals had been progressing, and the set was coming along, in spite of the distractions. The campus in general had not been aware of Marsha's disappointment and misfortune. Just as well—since the victim had unintentionally brought the trouble with her.

Jason Cabot called and asked me to come by the Security Office. He said that the Sarasota police had arrived and had been inspecting the sites of the assault. I asked how did they know where to look? He said that they had first-hand information: they had apprehended Dave Adams, who confessed and supplied details in return for certain incentives.

I hope that they didn't give away the whole farm, I thought as I made my way across campus.

I was introduced to the Sarasota police investigators who began filling me in. They admitted that they couldn't corroborate the Adams story because of the condition of the victim. I interrupted by commenting that I thought that Marsha was progressing nicely. One of the officers pointed out that they meant during the episode when she was incoherent.

"How and when did she become incoherent?" I asked.
"She had just driven back from Watkinsville."

"It didn't happen when she first returned," one of the officers replied. She had taken some of her clothes to the dorm, but when she returned, Dave Adams was in the back seat. He apparently had recognized her car from her living in Sarasota.

"How did he force her out of the car—at gun point?"

"No, with a stun gun! In fact, the entire sequence occurred with him in the back seat," the officer explained.

"How did she get to the lake, then?" I inquired.

"Apparently after the wounding, she was so groggy that in desperation he walked her to the lake before leaving in her car," he explained. "Not very smart," he added.

"What kind of punishment will the felon get?" I asked.

"More than a slap on the wrist," he replied. "There's car theft in addition to a felony."

"What about the neck wound?" I asked. "I understand that surgery is required."

"The family will likely bring suit against him," one of the officers added.

What a "spring" semester, and it has just started! There is some positive news to report. Our new freshman is on the road to recovery. Her ordeal was a blight on the entire campus: no campus is absolutely safe in spite of the most diligent security. It was good to have Harry and Darya at our beck and call. *Phaedra* promises to be one of our outstanding presentations, thanks to a brilliant director, a dedicated cast and crew, and the availability of a talented understudy. The Thomebeh Society has apparently decided to protect the extraterrestrial gift, and the campus has escaped the visit of another flying disk. Of course, perhaps the new models have indoor plumbing!